Bolivar's Heart

Bolivar's Heart

A Historical Novel

Margaret Donnelly

authorHOUSE®

AuthorHouse™
1663 Liberty Drive
Bloomington, IN 47403
www.authorhouse.com
Phone: 1 (800) 839-8640

Published by AuthorHouse 10/11/2019

ISBN: 978-1-5049-5863-9 (sc)
ISBN: 978-1-5049-5864-6 (hc)
ISBN: 978-1-5049-5865-3 (e)

Library of Congress Control Number: 2015917814

In memory of
Sabine García-Roady,
who belongs to Pacha K'anchay (Light of the Universe)

Other Books by Margaret Donnelly

The Spirits of Venezuela

Los espíritus de Venezuela

The Song of the Goldencocks

El canto de los gallos de oro

(Trafford Publishing)

The Path of Lord Jaguar

Bolivar's Heart

(AuthorHouse Publishing)

El corazón de Bolívar

(Editorial Sello Grulla)

ACKNOWLEDGMENTS

Old persecutions carried out by the Spanish empire in Latin America have survived to modern times. Some have bled into the connection between crime and migration, meaning the current abduction and transport of Latin American Indians to the United States and other countries as part of an international trafficking scheme. The past continues to mold the present.

The problem runs deeper because we fail to recognize that issues like human trafficking are anchored in our cultural memory. A culture of victimization, for instance, affects how we treat one another, exploiters and victims alike, and ineffectively manages our heritage and our resources.

So when I was in Santa Marta, Colombia, doing some ground research on Simón Bolívar and heard that Bolívar's heart was stored in the cathedral of that city, I wondered why that detail was important. In fact, Bolívar was the dean of a new vision in which Latin Americans weren't victims but the powerful by-product of what they inherited—*la nueva herencia*. Bolívar led us away from a culture of victimization. The information about the heart had more to do with our relatedness with this ancestor who had changed our lives forever in our continuing struggle to become powerful agents of change.

As I walked through the rooms of Santa Marta's Quinta de San Pedro Alejandrino, where Bolívar died, my local guide used a technique of speaking in the first person to take me into the womb of events surrounding that place in 1830. Suddenly I found myself listening to the guide's reenactment of a conversation with one of Bolívar's generals while Bolívar lay dying in the room next door. This experience was relived in Guanajuato while I followed the trail of Mexico's independence movement that was ignited by a priest, Miguel Hidalgo, in 1810. The tour guide of Teatro Juarez aptly described an inner dialogue with those who became the voice of change at that time, thus connecting me with those ancestors in a real, live way. I hope to convey the same passion for our history in this book.

The first individual who inspired me was Katia Gibaja, who seeded this conversation in 2006 while she served as a Quechuan consultant for the Museo de Arqueología de Alta Montaña in Salta, Argentina. Katia had followed the trail of Juan Bautista Condorcanqui, known as the last Incan king and brother of José Gabriel Condorcanqui, the precursor of Perú's War of Independence from Spain, to the famous cemetery known as La Recoleta in Buenos Aires, Argentina. Juan Bautista's 1825 letter to Simón Bolívar asking for permission to return to die in his beloved Cuzco, Perú, was never answered. Bolívar died on December 17, 1830.

Except for Juan Bautista's letter, which is a part of Argentina's historical archives, I had no academic document trail to follow, so I listened to the oral culture. Many persons offered very inspiring information about the unique legacy we've inherited in this continent, including the story behind Bolívar's heart and why Bolívar's answer to the Inca was written but never reached Juan Bautista Condorcanqui. Some of these individuals allege that the letter may have been destroyed by the Spanish establishment or someone who wanted to protect that establishment.

I'm indebted to my Colombian team, which includes Omar Cruz, German Cortes, Carlos Alberto Zuloaga, Luis Lara Sr. and his family, and Luis Eduardo Pinto Fuentes; my Venezuelan team, Violeta Matos and Rafael Gonzalez; my Mexican team, Roman Trujillo and José A. Guerra Aguilar; my US editors, the AuthorHouse team, Kimbriel Dean, and the person who designed the artwork of this book, John P. Bush; my friend Gregory Gomez; my life coaches,

Roy James and Vassa and Phil Neimark; Clara Hinojosa for inspiring me to create the character of Rafael Aguilar; Dr. Elizabeth Rojas, who traveled to Santiago, Chile, to get me Juan Bautista's memoirs, "Visión de los vencidos," edited by Hernán Neira; and Jacqueline Beer Heyerdahl, for her loving encouragement.

I can't thank my family enough for understanding my vision: Ines, my mother; my children, John and Veronica; my cousin, Janet. I'm also grateful to my professional team for taking care of my law practice while I birthed this book: Martina Aviles de Robles, Robert V. Torrey, Steve Mangum, John P. Bush, Guillermo A. García, and Almida E. Guevara.

CHAPTER 1

ISABEL CONDORCANQUI

Without water or food in the dark, windowless metal shed, Isabel settled into surviving the horrific, hot night, distracting herself with the sound of the flies crowding around the door for air. Nothing tempered the heat, only the heavy perspiration drops that ran down her scalp and thoughts of a fresh cupful of *café con leche* waiting for her in the morning. Thinking of something as simple as a café con leche distracted her from the dryness of her mouth, the hardness of the floor, and the heaviness of the metal brace around one of her ankles.

This was a good time to die, but she managed to defy those thoughts by removing her mind to the sacred mountains, the Apus, where, as a young girl, she had replenished herself in the festival of Qoyllur Rit'i. Her strength came from connecting with those mountains and the expectation that one day soon she would reunite with her brother, Antonio.

She fell asleep and dreamed with Antonio while they hiked together among the Apus to say a prayer to Pachamama, the mother. It was difficult to say a prayer. They were blinded by the light of Father Sun, so she grabbed Antonio's hand and followed his short, measured steps until he exploded into a run toward the edge of the mountain. She followed him.

Suddenly he turned around and, facing her, said, "They killed Pachamama!"

As soon as he stepped out of her dream, the door of the shed was yanked open, and two men grabbed her, one by the legs and the other by the arms. While one unlocked the ankle brace, the other slapped her. "Shut up, you whore! Shut up!"

She was too stunned to resist.

They dragged her back to the main house and threw her on the floor of the kitchen.

Suddenly her captors reacted to someone who was kicking down the front door. She was left alone. It was then that she decided to die.

CHAPTER 2

THE RETURN OF PACHAMAMA

Gloria Dolii García's eyes impatiently scanned the interior of the elevator. At that very moment, she was thinking of a human trafficking victim, a fifty-seven-year-old Peruvian woman whose name was Isabel Condorcanqui.

Gloria stepped out when the elevator door opened on the psychiatric floor of the hospital. Wary of being delayed, she quickly mapped out her way to Isabel's room. It wasn't the first time that she had been confronted with a bizarre case, but it was her first visit to a psychiatric ward.

A growing anxiety swept through her. The anxiety came from reviewing pieces of the government's record, Form I-213, which detailed Isabel's screams while blood gushed from her wrists, images that were difficult to suppress.

Isabel had cut her wrists after she was dragged out of a metal shed by two men. The shed was located in the backyard of a house in south Dallas. She had attempted to kill herself as soon as a unit of the Immigration and Customs Enforcement (ICE) surrounded the house where she and a group of men were held by Mexican smugglers. The arrest had occurred five days earlier. In the interim, her manic accusations against authorities far removed from the scene, both chronologically and geographically, landed her in the psychiatric ward of a Dallas hospital. Peruvian officials, she said, had kidnapped her.

Gloria held her breath but kept a cool composure with her briefcase gripped tightly and purse strapped around her shoulder as she came under the judgmental glare of the ICE officer who guarded the door of Isabel's room. Gloria's black hair was pulled back into braids that came together in a French *tresse* that cascaded to her waistline, held at the tip by turquoise beads. She was of short stature—borderline matronly as the mother of three grown children—with Navajo (Diné) features inherited from her full-blooded mother and gray eyes from her Anglo-American father. Hardworking and sharp yet soulful, she understood the trials of immigrants. She was handsome for her forty-five years, as her boss, David Levin, liked to say without realizing that honesty wasn't the best policy in the case of a woman's age. However, she never complained.

She pulled out a couple of plastic cards from her purse. The ICE officer inspected the passport ID card that identified her as a citizen of the United States and the other as a licensed attorney of the state of Texas.

He took another look at her, eyebrows close together, and dragged his glance back to the cards. As soon as he returned them to her, ready to inspect her briefcase and purse, metal crashing against glass vibrated the door. Within seconds, two nurses, a man and a woman, bolted around a corner of the hallway and moved swiftly by them through the door.

They had come from their monitoring station and tumbled into the room, where they confronted a small-boned woman clad in a light blue hospital gown with long, disheveled dark hair. Her eyes were fixed on the glass window that she had attempted to break. She continued to search for her reflection while the male nurse sidestepped the bed and grabbed the overturned metal stool from the floor.

From the doorway, Gloria noticed the white gauze around her wrists as the other nurse guided Isabel back to the bed.

Isabel refused the bed. "No. No. I need a mirror!" she screamed in Spanish, heaving with frustration.

"I promise that I'll bring you one," the female nurse said.

Isabel passed her hands over her hair, answering, "I must look at myself! Do you understand me? I need to see myself!" There were no mirrors in the room or in the private bathroom.

ICE Agent Gardner turned around. "The window is still holding. It's double paned. No serious harm done."

"I need a mirror!" Isabel screamed again as she was gently guided into one of the two metal chairs next to the bed.

The male nurse held the metal stool and said, "I'll take this away," meeting Gloria's eyes. "If you want to speak to her, go ahead. She has these episodes."

Gloria asked, "When can I speak to her physician?"

"Dr. Warner?"

"Here's my card," she offered. "Can you ask Dr. Warner to contact me as soon as possible?"

The man nodded, taking the card.

Gloria glanced at Agent Gardner, who smiled for the first time and said, "I'll be outside."

When everyone left the room, she pulled the other chair to her and sat down, facing Isabel. She extracted a writing pad from her briefcase and placed it on her lap. "Let's see ...," she said softly in Spanish, carefully absorbing Isabel's Mestizo face, round dark eyes, long nose, thin lips, and black hair that carried no hint of her age. She added, "My name is Gloria García. I've been informed that your name is Isabel Condorcanqui." However, Isabel made no eye contact, satisfying herself by keeping her hands folded in her lap while she stared down.

Gloria continued in Spanish. "I work for a law firm. The owner's name is David Levin. We agreed to represent you because the government of the United States wants to send you back to Perú."

A glint of movement seeped through Isabel's face although there was no hint of interest.

"Do you want to go back to Perú?" Gloria asked.

No answer.

She pressed on. "I need to know if there's any reason you shouldn't be returned to your homeland."

Isabel moved her head sideways but kept silent.

"There's a reasonable chance that we can get you asylum."

Her demeanor didn't change.

"I've been informed that you were held against your will in a house in south Dallas."

Her face remained frozen.

"And that you were taken to a shed in the backyard of the house where you were chained down overnight."

She shrank back in her chair but refused to react.

"A neighbor heard your screams and called the police. Is that what happened?"

According to the government's record, Isabel had been taken from the shed and returned by her captors to the main house every morning. Gloria added, "The authorities surrounded the house and were able to observe two men escort you out of that shed to the house early in the morning before ICE found you along with other undocumented aliens."

Isabel's breathing became labored.

"What kind of work did you do?" The possibilities included prostitute, cook, housekeeper, among many others. Isabel didn't have the air of a prostitute, like so many of them who showed up at local restaurants with male handlers closely watching over them. They were of varying ages but were mostly young, overly sexy with caked-on cheap makeup, like the puppets of a show. Isabel shared none of these traits. There was an aura of dignity about her in spite of her assumed status—enslaved domestic.

There was still no reaction.

Gloria tried the shock approach. "Why did you try to kill yourself?" It didn't work. She could sense Isabel's confused terror, so she reached into her purse and pulled out a pewter compact mirror. It had the head of a jaguar design on the cover. Isabel glanced at it. Gloria added, "It's a mirror. Open it."

Without taking it, Isabel stared at the design. "What animal is that?" she asked suddenly.

"It's a jaguar."

She glanced at Gloria with intense eyes. "You're a *gringa*. What's a jaguar to you?"

"The mirror was a gift. My husband gave the mirror to me."

"Puma is our symbol."

"A puma? Whose symbol?"

"The Quechua people," Isabel answered.

"I didn't know that."

"Why do you carry a jaguar with you?"

"It's a symbol of great power to many Mexicans."

"You aren't a Mexican. And where did you learn to speak Spanish so well?"

Gloria smiled. "My husband was Mexican. But I also learned Spanish from my clients."

"Mexican?"

"Yes," Gloria answered easily.

"The Mexicans treated me badly."

"I understand."

Isabel grabbed the compact and held it with both hands. "It's heavy," she said.

"It's pewter."

She managed a nod. She stroked the jaguar design with her fingertips. "And what happened to your husband?"

Gloria didn't like talking about it. However, she had to draw Isabel out. "He died."

"How?"

"He became very ill."

She nodded.

"Cancer," Gloria added.

"How long ago?"

"Six years ago."

*****

Isabel opened the compact, and her heart began to pound in her ears. Images of stone-faced men in uniforms racing in from all directions littered her head. She disconnected from her past. "I'm an old woman," she said when she glanced at her image.

"You still look beautiful," Gloria said, ignoring the wrinkles around her eyes and mouth. "Do you have any children?"

"I was beaten and raped so hard that my body couldn't carry another life."

Gloria gave her a nod of recognition. She continued. "So, tell me, who brought you to the United States?"

"They did."

"Who, exactly?"

Glancing around again, she shook her head. "I don't know their names. The same men who took me to Spain arranged things with some Mexicans."

"Where in Spain?"

"Ceuta."

"What were you doing in Ceuta?"

"Working."

"What kind of work?"

Isabel's mind tried to grab memories held back in her throat, so she swallowed and answered, "I worked as a maid and nanny."

"For how long?"

Her face was filled with sadness.

"Isabel, you need to help me," Gloria pleaded.

She relented. "I worked for the same family for more than thirty-five years."

"That's a long time." Gloria made a note on her pad. Would Spain take her, if not Perú?

"What could I expect?" Her breathing was slow. "I was a slave. I was kidnapped in Cuzco when I was seventeen years old."

"Tell me about it."

"I was born in Tungasuca, Perú."

Gloria pulled a legal-size document out of her briefcase and showed it to her. "This birth certificate says that you were born in Cuzco."

She shook her head. "My parents registered me in Cuzco, but I was born in Tungasuca."

"If you were a slave, how did you get possession of your birth certificate?"

Isabel didn't flinch, answering, "They gave it to me when I arrived in Mexico."

"Who had it before that happened?"

She shrugged. "The man I worked for in Spain."

"Who was the man?"

"A powerful man in Ceuta."

"In politics?" Gloria asked.

Isabel nodded. "Yes, a judge."

"Do you have any idea how he got your birth certificate?"

"No."

"How did your kidnappers know that you were Isabel Condorcanqui?"

"I had my school identification card in my pocket."

Gloria focused her eyes on Isabel's face. "So, how were you kidnapped?"

"I was pulled into a car in *centro* Cuzco."

"What were you doing there?"

"I was walking to a bus stop from a private school for girls. The school let us out at two-thirty in the afternoon, so it was soon after that."

"You belonged to a good family, then."

"My father was a merchant in Tungasuca. I was finishing my secondary education."

"What happened next?"

"They held a gun to my head, so I stopped screaming. Then they used something that smelled sweet that made me drowsy ..."

"Chloroform?"

"I don't know what it was."

"Where were you taken?"

"To an old jail."

"Where?"

"In Cuzco."

"How do you know it was in Cuzco?"

"It was like I was drunk, but I could tell where I was."

"How long did you stay there?"

"Two days, I think."

"What happened after that?"

"They took me to Pomacanchi."

"How did you know it was Pomacanchi?"

"I'm familiar with that area. I had a lot of relatives living there." She hesitated for a few seconds before she added, "My ancestral grandfather's house next to the *laguna* of Pomacanchi was burnt to the ground by the Spanish."

"Why?"

She arched her shoulders. "He was considered an enemy of the Spanish Crown."

"Was he?"

"Yes," she said with defiance.

"Where was your family?"

"My parents and my sister were in Tungasuca. Antonio, my brother, was also kidnapped. I never saw him again."

"Was he with you?"

She shook her head. "He was in another school in Cuzco."

"So how do you know he was kidnapped?"

"They told me."

"Were you kidnapped with others?"

"No. I was the only one they kidnapped. I was the only person in that jail." She shut her eyes, tormented by the memories, even though she realized that she was strangely desensitized. "From that jail," she added, "they took me to Pomacanchi and then to a nearby place where they forced me into a truck. There were more than one hundred of us herded into trucks and taken to Lima across the mountains."

"How old was Antonio?"

"He was fourteen years old."

"Was he part of that group?"

"No. I told you that he went to a different school and that I never saw him again."

"What else do you remember?"

"They put women and children together. There were many children and women, maybe sixty, and the rest were men, about fifty of them."

"Were they Indians?"

She nodded. "Mostly Quechua—a few were Aymara."

"Weren't you stopped by anyone on the way to Lima?"

"Yes, we were, but no one inspected the trucks. Our captors had official papers. We went through many towns."

"How did you know these towns?"

"They would unload us and give us water. The guards would say, 'We're in Huaytará,' or 'We're in San Vicente.'"

"Why were they taking you to Lima?"

"To load us on a ship."

"Once in Lima, what happened?"

"The ship went to Rio de Janeiro."

Gloria stopped writing, impressed by Isabel's remarkable memory, and glanced at her. "No one tried to escape?"

"How can anyone escape when he's starving?" she answered in a flat tone. "That's what they did. They also beat us."

"Did you spend any time in Rio de Janeiro?"

"Yes. I worked for a family for a year. They handed me over to my captors once their agreement was over."

"What agreement?" Gloria asked.

She bristled. "I was a slave. I only obeyed orders. That's when they shipped me to Spain, where the same thing happened again, because I was taken to Ceuta. That's how I got to Ceuta where I worked for that judge."

"That was a very long contract."

She nodded. "They needed me. I raised their children. But then the family had no use for me."

Gloria added a note in her pad: *Check into Stockholm Syndrome. Traumatic bonding.* She glanced up and said, "So, tell me—why didn't you walk away?"

She didn't answer.

"Your handlers were Peruvian, so did they stay in contact with you during all those years?"

"Yes."

"Did your employer know them?"

"Yes."

"Did they come to your house?"

"I lived with the family, so they visited that house."

"How often?"

She shrugged. "Every three months or so."

It was a surreal situation, but Gloria wasn't one to shy away from an instinctive feeling that Isabel was telling the truth. Gloria herself conjured up moments in her past that were hard to believe. She was Navajo, and no one outside of her immediate kin really understood what it was like to be Navajo. Capture bonding was universal among natives who had been sequestered by settlers, especially those who had fallen into the hands of Christian residential schools. Thousands of her Navajo brothers and sisters had adapted to the aggressors' culture, often forgetting or denying their own families. Such adaptive behavior guaranteed their survival, but it came with deep emotional scars. Therefore, she knew that safely tucked away in all of Isabel's sordid information was the truth. "So," she said, "you spent over thirty-five years in Spain, and no one bothered the judge."

She remained silent.

"Isabel, did you have any papers that allowed you to stay in Ceuta?"

"No."

"How did you get medical help?"

She shrugged. "The family's physician came to the house."

"You were in Spain all those years, and you never got any kind of identification card. Is that correct?"

"I was a slave," she answered evenly.

"So, how did you switch from Peruvian to Mexican handlers?"

"The Peruvians shipped me to Mexico."

"Without any papers?"

"They had my birth certificate. They gave it to me when I reached Mexico."

"Where in Mexico?"

"Veracruz."

Gloria blinked. She was familiar with that route. It was used to enter the United States through Brownsville, Texas. "Is that where the Mexicans got involved? Was it in Veracruz?"

Isabel nodded.

"For sure, you had contacts who could have helped you escape before you reached Mexico."

"I was afraid."

Gloria's mind sliced through the information to understand something that was incomprehensible to her. Isabel had languished in a prison with no locks, only beatings and fear.

"Why did you try to kill yourself before the Americans rescued you?" she asked.

"The Mexicans said that I would be put in a prison for entering illegally."

"Your captors are terrible people who placed you in a hot, small building night after night, without food or water. Why did you believe them?"

She shrugged. "I believed them."

Gloria managed a careful nod before she asked, "Can you go back to Perú?"

Isabel shook her head. "I was kidnapped for a reason. They took my brother and me."

"There's an issue that we call resettlement, meaning that you actually resettled in Spain. The government may try to return you to Spain."

Startled, Isabel's face froze. "I'm not a Spanish citizen," she said. "The Spanish destroyed my family."

Gloria glanced at her pad. *Delusional tendencies?* Dr. Warner would help her on this. She asked, "What happened to the rest of your family?"

"My parents and my sister were killed in a car accident sometime later." Weariness crossed her face.

"How did you find out?"

She answered dismissively. "They told me."

"When did you get this information?"

"I was on the ship to Spain."

"And what happened to your brother?"

She shrugged. "He got away."

"How do you know he got away?"

"They recently informed me of this."

"Do you know where he is?"

"He's in Colombia." A shadow lined her face. "At first, they told me that he was killed in Cuzco while he tried to escape when they tried to grab him." She sighed, tears streaming down her cheeks, and then added, "I agreed to come to the United States when they told me that he was alive in Colombia and that they would help me to find him."

Gloria frowned. "Why would they try to help you? Why would they tell you that after so long?"

She didn't answer, arriving at the same sobering realization. She reined in her confusion.

"Again, why would they help you find your brother after forty years?"

She arched her shoulders.

"Besides Antonio, are there other relatives?"

"No."

She was lying, and Gloria was aware of it. Peruvians had large extended families; however, she dropped the line of questioning and concentrated her gaze on her. "It's obvious that you're a victim of human trafficking, Isabel. So, where were your captors taking you? Did they tell you?"

"To Colorado."

"Colorado? Did they give you a name?"

"Victor."

"What's in Victor, Colorado?"

"They said that Victor has mines."

"What kind of mines?"

"I don't know."

"Why would you come through Dallas on the way to Colorado?"

"I don't know."

"Did they expect you to work in the mines?"

"No. I'm too old for that."

"For a family?"

"Maybe," she answered with a tone of resignation.

CHAPTER 3

DAVID LEVIN

With no word from Gloria, David Levin continued to confirm pieces of Isabel's story in his office through digital means. By midmorning, no clear answers had surfaced, except the painful reality that he had to follow Schopenhauer's advice: "Every man takes the limits of his own field of vision for the limits of the world." Indeed, all assumptions had to be pushed aside.

The top page of the government's record, Form I-213, listed Isabel's Subject ID number, personal description, photograph, left and right index fingerprints, birth date and birthplace, parents, occupation, and arresting information. Her father was Fernando Condorcanqui (deceased). Her mother was María Luisa Pacha (deceased). All the other questions that weren't answered on the top form were filled with the line, "See Narrative." Therefore, any reference to other members of her family—for instance, her brother, Antonio, and her sister, Maria—was included in the additional narratives in the back. No mention was made of her final destination in the United States even though the form noted that the city of embarkation was Ceuta, Spain.

The attached narratives started with an introductory paragraph. The investigation originated with a cooperating private individual (CPI), a neighbor who heard Isabel's screams from a backyard shed and contacted local law enforcement. The CPI wasn't fluent in Spanish but knew enough to understand a few words and determined that someone was being killed. Translated into English, the words "They killed Pachamama," reinforced probable cause.

The narrative gave details of her condition when she was arrested. The ICE agents found her on the kitchen floor of the house. The narrative went on. No removal proceedings were initiated due to the subject's potential role as a witness against her captors, who were part of a global slave trafficking network. In addition, as a result of information received from the subject, confirmed by US Attorney Karl Segal, the subject could be eligible to apply for asylum in the United States as a member of a particular persecuted social group: Condorcanqui, Túpac or Túpac Amaru.

The success of Isabel's case depended on tracking the history of her family back two and one-half centuries because it all started with the Great Rebellion of 1780, maybe before.

David really despised theories that required too much creativity, but he didn't like sacrificing it altogether because he appreciated the natural consequences of being human. While he worked on a set of facts at a time, he reminded himself of Schopenhauer's advice.

The main actors who started Perú's independence movement were Túpac Amaru II (José Gabriel Condorcanqui), the Catari brothers (Tomás, Dámaso, and Nicolás), and their relative, Túpac Catari (Julián Apaza), leaders of three rebellions that hit the region known today as Perú and Bolivia, between Cuzco and Potosí Mountain. They were all connected with individual touches, all fighting to regain control over their societies, which included familial and ancient trade relationships. The unrest had begun years before 1780 due to the increasing demands of the Spanish government—for instance, the *alcabala*, a sales tax on staples such as grains; the labor draft, or *mita*, which ripped fathers from their families and villages; and the *reparto*, forcing the natives to purchase or to produce European goods. In addition, church charges to burials and other sacred services were imposed, and the men who died in the mines were never returned and never received a communal mourning process. These ancestors were lost. Furthermore, Upper Perú was made a part of the viceroyalty of what is now Argentina, breaking up old trade patterns with Cuzco.

Overall, Aymara, Quechua, and other indigenous groups detested the deepening corruption of the Spanish *corregidores* and, worse yet, of their own caciques. They hated what the Spanish system had done to their society, especially to their women, the healers and priestesses and descendants of Mother Moon, Quilla, because they were pushed into insignificant roles in that society.

The leaders of the Aymaran revolt around Potosí Mountain and La Paz, Tomás Catari, and Túpac Catari, invoked their leadership from their positions as caciques. José Gabriel Condorcanqui, Túpac Amaru II, the leader of the Quechua around Cuzco, on the other hand, although a cacique, used his lineage as a direct descendant of the last official Incan king, Túpac Amaru I. These revolutionaries were all executed by the end of 1781 with the exception of José Gabriel's cousin, Diego Cristobal Túpac Amaru, who was executed in 1783.

But Pachamama? Who was Pachamama? Why did Isabel scream, "They killed Pachamama!"?

Tawantinsuyu, the Incan name for the Andean region that stretched from Bolivia, Ecuador, Chile, Perú, and northern Argentina, revered Pachamama as Mother Earth in ancient and in current times. According to their mythology, there was a pact between Inti, the Sun God, and the earth family, including Pachamama, who was considered his wife by some Andean groups.

Many didn't understand it, much less the divine's relationship with certain families like the transference process of Tibet's Dalai Lama. The flow of this human-sacred inheritance was interrupted by the invaders when Spain refused to build on the wisdom of the Andean people. Spain didn't follow the Roman concept of *utipossidetis*—the sacred cannot be possessed by an invading power.

David Levin pondered this for a few minutes. He looked forward to Gloria's report.

*****

Gloria and Isabel continued their conversation.

"I'm a descendant of José Gabriel Condorcanqui," Isabel said.

"Who's José Gabriel Condorcanqui?" Gloria asked.

"He was our ancestor," she answered, holding back a wave of paranoia. "José Gabriel was the great revolutionary."

A million questions swamped Gloria's mind, but she noted Isabel's sincerity. She replied, "I apologize for my ignorance, Isabel. I've never heard of him."

"His other name is Túpac Amaru II."

"Why does he have two names?"

"He dropped his father's name and adopted the ancestral royal name."

Gloria drew a deep breath. "What royal family are you talking about?"

"The Inca."

"Please keep in mind that I have to explain this story to the US government."

"José Gabriel was executed in 1781 in the main plaza of Cuzco."

"Why?"

"For leading a rebellion against the Spanish government. His hands and feet were tied to four horses, which tried to pull his body apart. When they saw they couldn't kill him that way, they cut his head off. His head was placed on a pike at the main door of Cuzco. His limbs were sent to different towns of the region, where they were shown. He was beheaded in the same place where our ancestor Túpac Amaru I was beheaded."

"Túpac Amaru I?"

"Yes, the last official Incan king."

"When was he beheaded?"

Isabel reached into her memory bank. "In 1572."

"There's no obvious connection between the beheading of this king and why you say you can't return to Perú," Gloria said. "It's impossible to imagine that the Spanish government would lock you up upon learning that you're a descendant of Túpac Amaru I. Spain doesn't govern Perú today. There has to be a recent history that supports what you're saying."

"I'm not a stupid woman, if that's what you mean," Isabel answered flatly. "I'm Quilla, the sister of Inti. I also went to private schools, so I had a good education and my family taught us to never forget our history. The Spanish have a very long memory, but so do we. Túpac Amaru I was the last official Incan king until José Gabriel claimed his rightful place. I'm *his* descendant. I'm the granddaughter of his brother, Juan Bautista. Maybe Spain doesn't care anymore, but there are powerful people in Latin America and Spain who *do* care that I'm around."

"Hundreds of years later?"

"We can prove it with official records." She stared at Gloria, who liked the defiance that was erupting from her. Isabel added, "The sun and the moon belong together. No one can deny their presence. That's why Inti and Quilla will never be destroyed in spite of what we've gone through. That's why José Gabriel claimed his rightful place after several centuries. No one can destroy *what is*. No one can destroy who I *am*."

Gloria nodded. "Please continue."

"José Gabriel's family was executed after he was killed, except for his two young sons and his half-brother."

Gloria glanced at the pewter compact on Isabel's lap, which she occasionally stroked. Isabel added in a low voice, "His brother, Juan Bautista, was exiled to Spain. I'm a direct descendant of Juan Bautista. As I told you, he's my ancestral grandfather."

"Can you prove what you're telling me?"

"Many books have been written about my ancestral uncle. My grandfather also wrote a book before he died."

"When did he die?"

"In 1827 in Buenos Aires. He's buried there. When he returned from his exile in Spain, he landed in Buenos Aires, but Simón Bolívar didn't allow him back to Perú."

"Simón Bolívar?"

"Yes."

"Didn't Bolívar like the Inca?"

"He didn't want my grandfather to return." She shrugged. "That's what they say."

Gloria paused in order to organize her questions. "Does your grandfather's book mention that he wasn't allowed to return to Perú?"

"No, but he wrote a letter to Bolívar."

"Have you seen this letter?"

"My parents spoke about it but told us not to discuss our family history because it was dangerous."

"What about Juan Bautista's descendants?"

"Why would he speak about them? That's why we survived. Many of my ancestors moved away from Cuzco."

"It's strange that he said nothing about his descendants."

"Juan Bautista was afraid."

"He died in 1827. Enough time had elapsed to make it safe for him to mention his kin."

"And get them assassinated? That's what you don't understand. As I said, everyone has a long memory. Forty years of exile didn't erase anything."

"Anything else?"

Isabel nodded and then began to sob.

Gloria grabbed a small towel from the bathroom, handed it to her, and leaned over and patted her shoulder. Minutes later, she returned to the chair and stared at Isabel in deep amazement. For a few minutes, she watched sunrays of the high morning waft in through the cracked window. Meanwhile, Isabel wrapped her arms around the towel and poured all the pain that she could manage into it.

Gloria gave Isabel time to cry before asking for more information. "What else should I know about your family?"

"My uncle's oldest son," she managed to say between sobs, "Fernando Condorcanqui, is buried in Spain."

"Where in Spain?"

"They say he's in Madrid."

"I'll investigate it."

"No one wants us to return."

Half-nodding, Gloria answered, "I wonder why Spain hasn't made an effort to return his remains to Perú."

"That's what you fail to understand. Powerful people want to bury our history, our heritage."

"But today is today, Isabel. We must prove that you're entitled to asylum, today."

"They don't want my family in Perú."

Gloria's intense attention focused on her. "I understand."

She nodded.

"Can we prove your ancestry?"

"My father's name should be enough," she replied, "but maybe you can trace it through official records."

"So, returning to the first issue I raised, because we need to be realistic, why would the Peruvian authorities persecute you now?"

Her mouth was tightly drawn, her breathing labored. "I don't know who they are, but there are powerful people who are still fighting against us. Please help me find my brother."

CHAPTER 4

CHASING THE FACTS

David Levin continued to chase after the facts. It was normal for him to spend hours planning out an important case, except that now he couldn't figure out why he had allowed Karl Segal to talk him into Isabel Condorcanqui's case. It was already high morning. His second-floor office was surrounded by stacks of files, Western art, and an extensive collection of Baroque music, which he listened to on a regular basis.

David's law firm was located in a Victorian house in Oak Cliff, an ethnically diverse neighborhood in south Dallas, equipped with a multipurpose library, one office used by Gloria, a reception area, and a kitchen on the first floor. The stairs led to five offices, including David's, a copier room, and two bathrooms. A swell of paperwork and equipment composed the organized chaos of this small firm.

US Attorney Karl Segal had called him a few days earlier to discuss the dilemma of removing a Peruvian woman who was arguably the sister of Antonio Condorcanqui, encouraging David to take her defense pro bono. Karl had never tried to talk him into anything in his thirty-year prosecuting career.

By now, David had already tracked down the name Condorcanqui and arrived at a pseudonym that connected articles sourced by Rafael

Aguilar, a Mexican journalist, and a Peruvian named Antonio, alias El Condor, the real source.

David found the third article of a series on the front page of *Revista Once*, a Buenos Aires human rights publication. The article covered the modern day's high volume of child labor networks arguably rooted in centuries of state-church slavery schemes. In more recent times, abductions of children during conflicts like the Dirty War used ideological grounds, taking these children from political prisoners and victims and placing them with conservative families through orphanages. The article implicated the Roman Catholic Church in this child-trafficking scheme. It had also stirred up a furious public reaction in Argentina, Chile, and Perú.

According to the article, "The best teacher is the Inquisition. The heretics of yesterday have morphed into today's subversives and hidden mass graves and missing children who can't trace their way back home."

David found a link to Antonio Condorcanqui, a former member of the MRTA, the Movimiento Revolucionario Túpac Amaru, which was a Marxist group in Perú that took its name from the legendary leader of the Inca people, José Gabriel Condorcanqui, known as Túpac Amaru II. The MRTA was considered a terrorist organization in the 1980s and 1990s until removed from the list in 2001.

The history of Rafael Aguilar was cleaner and clearer. He was from Venta Prieta in Hidalgo, Mexico. David knew a lot about Rafael's people, who were Otomí Jews. The file on Rafael had grown quickly. He had studied journalism at the Universidad Autónoma in Mexico City, followed by a master's at the University of Miami and a course in Cuzco. David also uncovered information about his eco-hotel in Turbaco, a small sleepy town outside of Cartagena, Colombia.

CHAPTER 5

THE FIRST ASSAULT

The first assault against Antonio and Rafael occurred when they were returning from Tenerife, a five-hour drive from Rafael's hotel in Turbaco, Colombia. This was their fourth joint venture to publish an article under the title, "Confessions of a Revolutionary, El Condor," this time by returning to the genesis of the bloody guerrilla movement that started in Uruguay and the more violent countercampaign that spread into Argentina, Chile, and other countries through Pinochet's Operation Condor.

Augusto Pinochet Ugarte, chief of the armed forces of the Chilean State, masterminded a geopolitical secret alliance from 1973 to 1980 that he and his allies named Operation Condor, although it became official in 1975, to destroy the world of Communism. The symbol of the condor was chosen because it was the national bird of Chile, Argentina, and Bolivia, members of the secret pact that also included Uruguay, Paraguay, and Brazil. All members engaged in tactics that included cross-border assassination using shared political data banks and terror. The campaign included improvised camps that carried out torture and summary executions. The targets were subversives and suspected subversives because none of these countries wanted left-wing radical movements, even the United States, which provided statistical and technical training and weapons support.

The purpose of their trip to Tenerife that morning was to interview a former underground fighter, now a retired merchant, who had been one of Antonio's guerrilla companions in Uruguay.

Operation Condor was now ancient history to many people. A lot of information had been declassified by the United States and other governments, but the roots of the insurrection ran deeper. Antonio wanted to trace that insurrection to his ancestor José Gabriel because the original Uruguayan guerrillas, the Tupamaros, had an Andean nativist rather than a Cuban agenda. Antonio was a young man in those days, so he enlisted his older friend in Tenerife to share his insights. The man had disguised his voice and no photos were taken, thus saving him any potential trouble.

Dusk was setting in when four armed civilians bearing semi-automatics jumped in front of Antonio's black, four-door Jeep and waved him to stop on the westbound shoulder of Ruta 80. They had parked their plateless silver Corolla on the shoulder, a strong indication that they were members of an informal police or military group who had waited for the Jeep while it headed back to Turbaco. It was brazen and well planned because the Jeep was the only car targeted by these civilians. They ignored the passing cars, buses, and trucks that slowly weaved around them with no intention of stopping and putting themselves in harm's way.

The glare of incoming traffic lights highlighted the rain hitting the windshield. Nonetheless, Antonio's trained eyes stayed focused on the assailants' covered faces. When they pointed their semi-automatics at him and ordered him and Rafael out of the car, it was natural for Antonio to react quickly. He raised his arms and stepped out, but, instead of giving them the keys, he threw them over his shoulder as far as he could into the dense vegetation that edged the road, scaring the thieves, who promptly transferred the stolen recording equipment, cameras, phones, and overnight bags into the Corolla. They left Antonio, his Jeep, and Rafael behind unscathed.

A light rain continued to hit the unlit road, making it slippery but not as dangerous as the robbery that they had just experienced. However, Antonio didn't waste any time before moving into action.

His deep, large, black eyes, set under strong eyebrows that arched at the end, immediately focused on the Jeep's secret hole in the glove compartment, and he quickly extracted another set of keys while Rafael took notice without a comment.

He inserted the new key in the ignition, his eyes already locked on the two-lane, asphalt road ahead. The Jeep roared into hot pursuit of the four men who had performed a classic Colombian roadside armed assault.

He pushed the gas pedal to the floor while searching for the faint glimmer of familiar taillights to appear around a curve. He didn't want to outrun the thugs, just to follow them, if and when he found them. He suspected they were returning to Cartagena. In the meantime, Rafael's talkative personality relented to the tension inside the Jeep. Rafael was forty years old but looked older and, compared to Antonio, was heavier and taller, a Mexican with a darker bronze complexion, more indigenous-looking than European.

"Those semi-automatics are used by my Colombian antiterrorism colleagues," Antonio mentioned.

Rafael nodded. "They're looking for information."

"They're going to dissect our phones."

Rafael laughed. "And they'll be speaking with every magazine and newspaper between here and Canada."

"And your family in Venta Prieta."

Antonio seldom spoke about his family or about his miraculous escape from being kidnapped but said enough to Rafael to emphasize the reason for working for DIRCOTE. "After years of fighting, I had to join the enemy in order to survive," he said, also divulging the fact that he was already working for the Peruvian government when they had met in Cuzco.

"What about your family?" Rafael asked ruefully, suspecting that it was the time to pry this information out of him. "You never talk about them."

He didn't answer.

"Surely, you have a living relative who wants to hear from you."

"My sister," he said in a flat tone.

"What's her name?"

"Isabel."

"Is she older or younger?"

"Older."

"Where does she live?"

"I don't know."

Rafael sensed that Antonio was battling against demons of some kind. "So, when was the last time you saw her?"

"Forty years ago."

"What happened?"

"She was arrested a few hours earlier. She told them where they could find me. She betrayed me."

"How do you know that?"

He didn't answer.

"And you believed them?" Rafael answered. Antonio's myopia really irritated him. He added, "You know, I could try to comfort you, my friend, but I'm not going to do that. You're chasing after a lie, or the lie is chasing you. Have you made any effort to track her down?"

"Yes. A few years ago, a colleague in DIRCOTE did a search and told me that she was in Ceuta."

"Ceuta, Spain?"

"Yes."

"What else did you find out?"

"That she was working for a judge."

"Why didn't you look for her?"

"I did, recently. In fact, three months ago I found out that the judge had died and that she was no longer in Ceuta."

"Any idea where she could be?"

"I don't know. She evaporated. Maybe she's dead."

Rafael ruminated the information.

Antonio changed the subject. "Did they take your wallet?"

"They did," Rafael answered. "What about yours?"

"Mine is hidden in the back."

"Care to tell me about your other secret compartments?"

"This Jeep belonged to a notorious drug trafficker."

Rafael laughed. "I won't publish that information."

"I'm a legal resident of this country with good friends in Perú, and you're a famous writer."

They pressed on. His expectation of catching the Corolla had vanished. He had to think ahead. Rafael's hotel in Turbaco was thirty minutes away. He glanced at Rafael and asked, "So, what are you going to do about your wallet?"

"My passport and other credentials are in a safe at the hotel. Meanwhile, keep a watch for that Corolla. It'll surface somewhere."

He nodded.

"Hope they don't surprise you again. You're the one who lives there."

"Interesting they waited for us on Ruta 80."

"They followed us to Tenerife this morning."

Antonio remained silent.

It was Rafael's turn to change the subject. "I'm leaving for Mexico City in a couple of days."

"And I'm moving to Santa Marta."

"When?"

"When my divorce is final."

Rafael focused on what was important. "Our last article stirred things up."

"I didn't reveal anything that would get me in trouble with anyone except other guerrillas, and most of them are either dead or in prison."

"The magazine is still receiving irate letters."

"People don't want to face the skeletons," Antonio said.

"What about someone in the Peruvian government?"

"I was an employee of the Peruvian National Police for a long time and a guerrilla fighter before that. I know about sabotage. I'm not sabotaging anyone. They're looking for information. What kind? I don't know."

"They're still prosecuting former members of the MRTA, Antonio, even if it's not considered a terrorist organization today."

"Yes, but I know things that you don't, and I don't pose a threat," he lied.

CHAPTER 6

ANTONIO AND RAFAEL

Antonio was extremely agile for his fifty-four years, a thin, medium-boned man with a prominent nose like an eagle's beak, thin lips, penetrating black eyes, and graying long hair that he pulled into a ponytail. His high cheekbones and square forehead bore a striking resemblance to his famous ancestor, José Gabriel Condorcanqui.

Many said that Antonio reminded them of José Gabriel, even though he disputed this comparison, maybe out of humility. Much of his behavior came from his Quechuan sense of survival, for sure. He liked to say that his quick reactions were a by-product of the experience he gained when he was kidnapped by paramilitary troops at the age of fourteen; when he did combat time as a member of the guerrilla movement, including the MRTA; and more recently, when he was an informant of the antiterrorism division of the Peruvian National Police, also known as DIRCOTE, and reached an agreement with the government of Perú to avoid prosecution when the MRTA was dropped from the terror organization list in 2001.

Antonio was a present-day example of Bolívar's spirit, a radical thinker akin to a wave that was about to break at the end of a very dark tunnel. He was fearless, independent, and persistent, and he had great stamina—key ingredients for his resilience.

Upon retiring from DIRCOTE, he broke his silence and began sourcing articles in the prestigious Argentinian human rights magazine *Revista Once.* The articles challenged the establishment even though no one really clearly knew, or could say, who or what the establishment was. Nonetheless, the articles were a strike against the centuries-old persecution of dissenters, perceived or real, motivated by the thirst for power or greed of special interest groups. Each article, in fact, tackled historical facts as a part of an information war because, according to Antonio's view, information was a rare commodity in Latin America.

Antonio and his ally, Rafael Aguilar, aptly used the alias El Condor because Antonio was the primary source of the facts. In addition, the alias had far-reaching consequences not only because Perú's poor, indigenous communities fed a rising wave of slave traffic of children and women but also because these communities had a strong mythological relationship with the all-seeing condor. It was also a way to avoid using Antonio's famous paternal name, Condorcanqui, although it was known to his colleagues in DIRCOTE, who no doubt transferred a copy of his file to Colombian authorities when he retired from his government job and moved to Colombia.

Antonio's solid friendship with Rafael had begun over ten years earlier when they had participated in a short-term journalism course in Cuzco. Their respective ancestries brought them together as natural allies. Antonio was a local Quechua, a descendant of one of the first anti-Spanish revolutionaries of the Andes, while Rafael was an Otomí from Venta Prieta in Hidalgo, Mexico. Antonio was the Andean condor, and Rafael was the Mexican eagle. Both belonged to groups traditionally persecuted by the Spanish government through the Inquisition, a police state at war with the world, especially against the Indians. Rafael Aguilar was also a Jew; in fact, he was an Indian Jew.

After finishing their course in Cuzco, they went their separate ways and dedicated themselves to different goals. Antonio returned to Lima, eventually making his way to Colombia by marrying a woman from Cartagena, while Rafael continued to make his mark as a freelance journalist for high-end magazines and newspapers in Mexico and the United States. He found an opportunity to expand his financial horizons by investing in a hacienda in Turbaco, which he converted into a hotel.

They found their opportunity to reconnect when Rafael received a grant to do an article on the human trafficking industry of Latin America. He was aware that Antonio knew a lot about the subject because he had spoken about it frequently in Cuzco, so he searched for and located him in Cartagena. Antonio was retired from the intelligence business and now doing research on Simón Bolívar.

Antonio was digging into the city's extensive archives for any references on an important, very personal subject, an elusive letter dictated by Bolívar in the last days of his life. The letter said that his heart should be buried in Cuzco. It was not only newsworthy; it was deserving of a book written by a living descendant of José Gabriel Condorcanqui and Juan Bautista Condorcanqui. It was also a way to work with the past in an organic way. It transcended the boundaries imposed by historians, who, for the most part, never understood the Andeans' relationship with their own heritage or Bolívar's extraordinary connection with them. No one had more right to write it than Antonio Condorcanqui.

Writing a book about Bolívar's heart remained in the back of their minds, but it took a backseat because their articles were more important. They underlined modern agendas seeded by the past organizations, like the Inquisition, whose alter egos played a different role but the same purpose.

According to the articles, the colonial framework that the Spanish conquerors designed continued to suffocate the living world of local communities, especially those who were indigenous. The modern persecutors were private and government groups rather than ecclesiastical ones that occasionally presented themselves in the guise of modern Truth and Reconciliation Commissions, measures of appeasement with an apologetic agenda that had sprung up over the years to deal with the victims of various wars against humanity. However, too many things were left buried, unsaid and unresolved, about the thousands upon thousands of unclaimed skeletons as far north as Canada and as far south as Argentina and Chile, too many souls who screamed for justice, to bring closure for their families and their communities. The court of public consciousness could not ignore those persecuted in recent times.

Antonio and Rafael claimed that the expungement strategies that had started centuries ago with a religious theme of targeting potential heretics had morphed into today's secret police state. The targets of yesterday had become the suspected subversives of today, the ghosts haunting Dawson Island in Chile and of those buried in the Indian residential schools of Canada.

In fact, one of their articles explained how few things had changed. "The most famous purification trial occurred in Lima, Perú, as early as 1635 against one hundred suspected Jews who were publicly tried and murdered by the church with the approval of the civil authorities. Today, the persecutors get a confession from the target, and then they impose solitary confinement and torture, a so-called trial, followed by execution. Then as now, these tactics strengthen the domination of modern interest groups such as the mining industry assisted by political and military allies."

Chapter 7

TURBACO

At six o'clock on the following morning, Rafael lifted himself from the double bed, ready for a day of hurried organizing. After he peered from his open balcony and looked over the hills that protected the hacienda's western perimeter, he went into the adjoining bathroom and took a quick shower. While he shaved, he welcomed one of his housekeepers, José, who had knocked on the door.

Not one to interrupt his boss at this time of the day, José quietly left freshly ironed blue jeans and a long-sleeved cotton shirt on the bed next to a large, empty suitcase. José retired downstairs to the kitchen to wait for his boss because Rafael preferred to eat his meals in the seclusion of the terrace outside the kitchen, away from the hotel's guests, who always used the communal kiosk in the back. Rafael wasn't well disposed to any kind of conversation before breakfast.

Meanwhile, Rafael silently stared at his face in the bathroom mirror. His flat, wide forehead and strong eyebrows came together in a gentle scowl, the result of quietly chastising himself for not insisting that Antonio spend the night here. After dropping him off, Antonio had smiled coolly and driven away in his Jeep.

Rafael lathered his square jaw and slightly dimpled chin and then raised the fleshy tip of his long nose to cover his upper lip with shaving cream, distracting himself with menial thoughts. As he did often, he wondered whether he should grow a beard, but logic always seemed to override this question. A beard detracted from the image of a veteran journalist, and in the forum of public opinion, appearance was an important factor. Plus, most of the men in his family didn't like to grow their facial hair, even a mustache.

His eyes, which were brown and set wide apart, assessed the dark bronze color of his skin and his square torso under narrow shoulders, advertising his strong Otomí roots. On the other hand, his height, five feet and eleven inches, and abundant, wavy black hair were classic Castilian features, an attractive balance for a man who easily maneuvered his way through Mexico and Colombia. He was single in spite of a string of relationships, which often ended because of his travels.

He finished shaving. He packed his suitcase, a task he never delegated to anyone, and then joined José and his wife, Amalia, who were the administrators of the hotel, a two-level, white, concrete building with Colombian mahogany ceilings, polished tile floors, and a cobbled courtyard in the center.

With Antonio in his thoughts, he ambled through the courtyard, which was surrounded by bedrooms offering outside balconies and terraces bounded by woodlands that typically shadowed the immediate countryside. The five-hectare spread did not lack the intrusions of abundant wildlife, like caimans, boa constrictors, monkeys, parrots, ducks, native turtles, and iguanas, held at bay or controlled by a massive ten-foot wall around the immediate periphery and José's gun-toting inspections.

The spread had previously been the country estate of a local top-tier drug financier now serving prison time in Germany. It was wrapped by heavily forested land with tema, totumo, tamarind, and palm trees on two sides; a spacious lawn with a kiosk where guests were served meals in the back; and a small swimming pool fed by a natural hot spring on the eastern side.

The tropical lushness added a colorful contrast to the black ironwork of the balconies and the gate that protected the grounds from the road that passed by in the front. Although modern, the architecture was consistent with the Spanish colonial architecture of the area, especially Cartagena, six kilometers away.

After breakfast, Rafael toured the property with José to organize the ordinary affairs related to the upkeep of the hotel before leaving on his trip. As usual, José worried that the canopy of trees around the kiosk needed attention, as well as the thatched roof with an overhang that kept the downpours from ruining the polished floor of the kiosk. These simple protections from the weather became more important with the approaching rainy days of August.

While José talked, Rafael's trained eyes scanned the tropical dishes on six rectangular guest tables—rice, plantains, steak, fish, black beans, fruit, yucca—a Colombian-Mexican (Otomí) menu that most guests found delightful. Meanwhile, they continued their inspection toward the eastern side of the property while Rafael rattled off orders until José, who was a fifty-year-old retired member of the local police force, said, "Señor Rafael, excuse the impertinence, but I noticed that your overnight bag is missing."

Rafael stopped in front of the thermal pool and took on the task of explaining what had happened the night before.

José plainly conceded to what was apparent. "Antonio has a past that may be catching up with him, don't you think?" José reminded Rafael of his father, except that his father was Otomí and José was very European-looking. José's lean face had thin lips that parted slightly, and although his features were unremarkable, he sported a patrician face under a mane of grayish hair. He had proven to be a hardworking, solid employee who never pretended to be what he wasn't.

Rafael shook his head. "Antonio worked for the Perú National Police, José. He's retired like you are."

"Yes, but the articles …"

"Those articles are about the Túpac Amaru Revolutionary Movement, which has been disbanded. Antonio became a member of the National Police after that."

"But there are people who are still alive who may be implicated by the articles."

Rafael shrugged. "All he wants to do is to write a book about Bolívar."

"Bolívar?"

"How dangerous is that?" Rafael sat down in a lawn chair and waved at José to do the same. Both stared at the tear-shaped, multilevel pool not more than two yards away, which was fed by an impressive cascade of hot water drawn from an underground spring. The pool had been a natural pond before the current house was built. The former owner didn't touch the natural waterfall that seeped through the rocks and built a pool in order to keep sediment from building up.

In addition, the chairs were ten paces from a tamarind tree with branches that drooped from a crown that was sixty feet high. From the width of the trunk, local scientists determined that the tree was probably already fifty years old when Bolívar visited Turbaco in 1830. By now, it had reached priestly ancestral status, as José liked to say, and watched over everyone like an elder who oversaw the activities of his grandchildren.

"Maybe the articles are making someone very mad," José insisted. He added, "As I said, some people never forget and never forgive."

Rafael nodded as he checked his wristwatch. "When I reach Mexico City, I'll call you from there. I want you to keep an open eye for any suspicious activity. They stole my wallet."

"What did your wallet contain?"

"My Mexican identification card and driver's license and one credit card, but I'll replace them in Mexico."

CHAPTER 8

THE SECOND ASSAULT

While sunrise started to edge in through the balcony door of his small apartment in downtown Cartagena, Antonio, who usually expressed his emotional landscape while asleep, dreamed that he was standing on the summit of Cerro Rico. He was searching for a way to bring back something lost by his people.

Enough evidence had lent support to the folklore that the mountain was haunted by the spirit of Pachamama. It was the dwelling place of the Sacred Mother of the Quechua and Aymara people, and it always brought strong reactions, from an emotional paralysis to an outburst of tears. This magnetic presence made Cerro Rico one of the most popular reminders of the connection between the divine and the earth, the past and the present.

Dreams about the mountain, otherwise known as Potosí Mountain, also triggered some kind of memory at a deeper level, sometimes in the form of the stairway that took Antonio in two opposite directions, up or down. Running up to the rooftop away from soldiers waiting for him outside of his school in Cuzco forty years ago meant heaven because that's how he had outmaneuvered them. He remembered the Indians who were forced down into the bowels of Potosí Mountain and had no way to escape hell, a reminder of the phrase that each Spanish peso cost the lives of ten Quechua and Aymara Indians, drawn from sixteen provinces of colonial Perú.

The dream today triggered a strange sense of relief, however, because of the presence of his ancestral uncle, José Gabriel Condorcanqui. José Gabriel told him that something would stretch him beyond his boundaries and lead him to a mission that would lift the heart of his people.

Suddenly his uncle told him to run, and he woke up and sat on the edge of his bed. His sensitive hearing caught soft footsteps on the stairs that were real enough to awaken him. By then, light was filtering into his apartment, which had one room, one bathroom, and an adjacent kitchen on the top floor of a three-story building.

He made his way over to the closed curtains behind the balcony. He peeked through a crack in order to assess any movement on the street below. His eyes fixed on a civilian man on the opposite sidewalk who pointed at someone or something and appeared to be directing an action. Then the man's gaze swung upward and locked on Antonio's balcony. Immediately, Antonio knew that he had no time to spare. His bare feet ran across the cold tile floor, and he barricaded the front door with a sofa and then grabbed his knapsack. It was already packed.

He had expected this assault. Therefore, as he mentally mapped his planned escape route, he dressed, laced up his tennis shoes, ran to the kitchen, and pushed out the metal screen of the window located over the sink. As soon as the screen released and fell onto an adjacent rooftop, he jumped on the windowsill. From there, he stood up just as he heard the sound of something hard being slammed against his door, maybe boots or the butts of rifles. He swung the knapsack over him onto a steel beam that supported his roof. Seconds later, his hands grabbed the same beam, and with all the strength that he could muster, he pulled himself up until he was able to crawl away to an abutting building, sending pieces of red tile down below. He was dripping with sweat.

Minutes later, soldiers shouted threats through the window behind him, but it was too late. He knew the territory of Cartagena, especially the neighborhoods around Plaza Bolívar, which offered plenty of balconied structures with an abundance of open courtyards with marble or stone stairs that descended into doors. Doors like these always spilled into a congested warren of narrow streets.

Glancing around furtively, he shuffled past pedestrians and peddlers huddled against one another. He walked away from the heavily guarded city center. Once at a safe distance, a gale of emotions swept through him while he analyzed the telltale signs that he was the object of a local manhunt. He took a taxi to Manga Island.

"Where in Manga Island?" the driver asked.

Taxi drivers were informants, so Antonio knew better than to reveal his true destination. "Corner of Calle 25 and Carrera 17," he answered. He would walk to the old fort that served as the situs of a restaurant that doubled as a marina. He knew the assistant manager of the restaurant, Jorge Vargas, an expatriate like himself who had married a Colombian woman. Like most of his most trusted friends, Jorge had been involved in the intelligence community before moving into the hospitality business.

Once at the corner, Antonio followed his instincts. He tucked his cotton plaid shirt into his faded jeans, giving no hint of his situation, and calmly walked west toward the waterfront, watching out for suspicious men in civilian gear. They could be anywhere. He was relieved that he had no phone with a signal that could be tracked down.

With no hesitation, he had left the Jeep in a friend's private garage the night before and stashed everything worth anything in his backpack, including cash and a false Colombian passport that would serve as his cover until he could resurface again as Antonio Condorcanqui.

The friend who had agreed to keep his Jeep had provided the best safe haven because the vehicle was inside of a boutique hotel, a former colonial convent in the heart of Cartagena. His friend was the owner of the hotel and also a master of discretion. He didn't ask where he was going, nor did Antonio offer any information except to say, "Watch for any messages from Mama Quilla."

"Not El Condor?"

He shook his head. "In case you forget, she's the sister of our Sun God."

"I won't forget."

"If you have any messages for me, use the classifieds of *El Universal*. I'll do the same."

"Done, amigo."

He would use another code name for Jorge Vargas, who probably was preparing for the restaurant's lunchtime rush. Time was moving rapidly. It was already ten o'clock when he scrambled up to the old fort and reached the gate of the restaurant. He kept himself in check. His eyes scanned the main door until Jorge walked over toward him.

"Good to see you," he said, shaking Antonio's hand.

"Can we talk?"

Jorge nodded. He sensed trouble. After instructing the staff not to interrupt him, he took Antonio to a table in the outermost part that edged the water. The area was safe—it was empty. "The lunch crowd will begin to arrive soon," he said. "Please sit down. Would you like anything to eat ... drink?"

Antonio shook his head, unloading his backpack unto a chair, and sat down. "I'm in a hurry. I have to get out of town."

"Where do you have to go?"

"Barranquilla." Once there, he planned to stop by the archdiocese's office before taking a bus to Santa Marta. He added, "I can't leave Cartagena by land."

"I can get you a small yacht at a great discount."

"How soon?"

He hunched his shoulders and reached for his phone inside his coat pocket.

Antonio frowned. "Use the land line, please."

Jorge pulled his hand away. "As you say, my friend."

In a muted tone, Antonio added, "My guess is that the articles must have made someone angry."

"I read those articles."

"What do you think?"

Jorge shrugged. "When you accuse anyone of child-snatching schemes, you have to expect trouble."

"Think about it," he argued.

"About what?"

"It's more than that, Jorge. When some people torture and murder others, rip their children away in order to reprogram them, dump people in mass graves, what is all that telling us?"

"Everyone wants to protect his assets, whether they're financial or political," Jorge argued. He added, "It's always the Inquisition, Franco, or Pinochet when it isn't some other deluded elite group. We've had the same damn teachers. Operation Condor may have been implemented by Pinochet, but the same networks existed before 1975 and afterward. When you speak as El Condor, you're going to get people even more upset. People want to remain ignorant. It absolves them of any responsibility."

Antonio remained silent.

Jorge pursued this point. "Didn't you expect this?"

Antonio gave him a small nod.

"I know you're using the articles as a platform, but tone down the inspiration. Bolívar could afford to issue manifestos and engage in superhuman military acts. He was rich and young. Today, you're dealing with another, maybe more powerful, group with runaway agendas."

"Yes, off the political grid and going after global resources." Antonio glanced at his wristwatch, adding, "Send messages to me through *El Heraldo*. I'll do the same. Use the code name of Inti." Jorge was familiar with the creation myth of the Inca in which the sun and his sister, the moon, or Quilla, created the founder of the Inca, Manco Cápac.

Jorge didn't waste another second to ask about his plans. "What's in Barranquilla?"

"The Inquisition. There's a letter that I need to get."

"About what, if I may ask?"

"About Bolívar's heart."

Jorge listened.

Antonio continued, "Very few know about this letter. There's a Dominican priest who has a copy. It was signed by Bolívar and witnessed by Alexandre Prospère Révérend, his de facto physician, and it states that Bolívar's heart should be buried in Cuzco. Révérend apparently followed Bolívar's instructions. The heart was placed in a coffer and transferred to the Cathedral of Santa Marta. However, the original letter was hidden or lost, and nothing was done to transfer the coffer to Cuzco. As I said, there's a Dominican priest who has a copy of that letter."

He paused before continuing. "Révérend was probably aware of the ancient Egyptian belief that every human heart appreciates the intelligence of the soul. The Egyptians never destroyed the heart. That argument aside, the letter is consistent with Bolívar's deep, emotional connection with our native people, which, in Révérend's view, had to be preserved. He may have separated it but trusted the church authorities of Santa Marta to send the heart to Cuzco."

"You believe the original letter is in Barranquilla?"

"Maybe. I don't know whether Révérend kept the letter or gave it to someone else, but the Dominican's copy appeared legitimate. In fact, the coffer stayed in Santa Marta when Bolívar's bones were transferred to Caracas twelve years afterward."

"How did you find out about its existence?"

"A historian from Santa Marta. However, I need to track the priest down." Saying this, Antonio stood up.

"Okay, amigo, I'll make the call," Jorge said.

"I'll walk around and keep an eye on the dock," Antonio said, picking up his backpack and, in sobering silence, directing his attention to the grounds behind a row of old canons.

*****

Antonio was very aware that Perú's was a complex society still tormented by its bloody, obtrusive past, which paralyzed everyone into a state of deep, emotional numbness. José Gabriel's only child who had lived, Fernando, still lay buried in Madrid, and the remains of his half-brother, Juan Bautista, rested in La Recoleta in Buenos Aires. A succession of governments of Perú had tuned them out of the country's history, though they honored José Gabriel Condorcanqui, or Túpac Amaru II.

Antonio's chest tightened as he concentrated his gaze on the cruising yachts beyond the seawall, wondering how soon his own would dock. A pain throbbed at the back of his head, so he alleviated his discomfort by sitting on the wall and watching the waves pound the coastline.

Meanwhile, he mulled over the dream's hidden messages. Maybe the dream had tapped into Bolívar's relationship with the history of Potosí Mountain. On April 13, 1825, Bolívar's commander in High Perú, Antonio José Sucre, won the last battle against the Spanish outside of Potosí, one the greatest assets of the Spanish empire due to its silver mines. Only a few days before the battle, Bolívar started his journey along the coastline of Perú toward Cuzco, which he reached on June 25. According to a letter he wrote on the following day, he was aware that he had arrived at the country of the Sun of the Inca, both fabled and historical. He described their stone monuments, great streets, pure customs, as well as genuine traditions, stating that no one had any idea or model or copy of their social creation.

It was no accident that Juan Bautista had written to him from Buenos Aires one month before Bolívar reached Cuzco. Bolívar had set out to learn how the native Peruvians lived. Juan Bautista acknowledged Bolívar as "The Liberator." As an eighty-six-year-old man, he wanted to return to die in his native country. But Bolívar never answered him.

Antonio doubted that Bolívar intentionally ignored Juan Bautista or, if he did, it was for the purpose of protecting the last heir of the Inca kings. Bolívar was mindful of the Inca's great history and took note of their poor living conditions; however, most of all, he was also aware that Perú and High Perú, later Bolivia, had a divided society, especially among the creoles, who could easily betray Juan Bautista.

Soon after Bolívar visited Cuzco, he abolished the Indian labor tribute to the Spanish Crown, or the mita, always abused by the

Spanish. In fact, the Inca had begun that tributary system, but the Spanish took advantage of it without any decent limits. The Inca's expansion during the fifteenth and early sixteenth centuries under the guidance of Cuzco was based on labor: they needed to obtain workers to build their great road system and to serve as soldiers, thus uniting a very diverse ecosystem under a code of economic exchange and gifting, at the heart of which was the law of *ayni*, or reciprocity. It was the code of *pax incaica*, or Inca Peace, a worldview that was inclusive, innovative, and practical and that put Cuzco and its minority rulers, the Inca, at the center of the Andean universe they governed. They astutely incorporated the elite of local communities into the imperial elite, thereby establishing a network of bloodlines for authority as well as for an economic advantage that relied on the secure flow of labor and goods and the solid protection of their frontiers.

Ayni wasn't a concept. It was a way of belonging to this world while connecting every individual to his divine purpose. Antonio knew this. He was searching to give his people the prestige they deserved. With the arrival and imposition of Spanish values, however, Andean native values were challenged. Pachamama was about community and family, the family of the Andes and of the Americas, but these values had been forced into a deep sleep.

Antonio sensed that Bolívar had been aware of all of these things. Therefore, when Bolívar mentioned that no one had any idea or model or copy of the Inca's social creation, he knew what they had made. Countless Andean communities had supplied thousands of llamas to the Inca. The llamas were key to the Inca's global transportation and military system, which is why Bolívar recognized their value and had given orders to save them from extermination. He had also issued an assortment of decrees dealing with commerce, trade, agriculture, mining, education, and hygiene to help Antonio's ancestors.

While Antonio inspected the sea traffic, his emotions swung between calm and despair. On one hand, he felt some consolation that he had tried to locate Isabel, yet, on the other, he was angry that she had betrayed him, making no effort in forty years to contact him. In addition, he couldn't allow what was happening to undermine his resolve to continue publishing articles and, above all, to find Bolívar's letter. The dream about Potosí Mountain was just about that. The dream called him to go up to the summit of the mountain to challenge the tyranny of the past and lift the heart of his people.

CHAPTER 9

SOUL POWER

David paid no attention to the early afternoon heat and sprinted out of his house on South Bishop Avenue, and jogged north toward the arts district. Once he reached the northern east-west perimeter of the district through its assorted antique, art, clothes, food, and tattoo establishments, he opted to momentarily focus on a code enforcement patrol car parked across the street. No doubt the officer was searching for pink yard art, stray dogs, and weed-covered gardens. The rational logic of the local Caucasian culture didn't favor weeds or anything that didn't fit into their own definition of order.

A city officer in his early to midthirties who obviously was of western European descent was arguing with a Latino man in his forties. It appeared that the argument was heated because the Latino man looked very agitated. His raised arms pointed to the other houses on the street. The officer kept peering around the front yard of the Latino man's house, located north of the parking lot of Firehouse 15, a local landmark that was home to a very popular Mexican-Salvadoran restaurant.

David wasn't blindly opposed to the gentrification of Oak Cliff because it attracted members of the middle and upper-middle classes. But he also valued diversity, which meant preserving the area's African American, Asian, and Latino blue-collar influences.

In fact, he knew many of the families who lived in the old houses on Bishop Avenue, like the Latino man whose home the code officer was carefully inspecting. Half of the homes belonged to immigrants whose concept of art, particularly garden art, was very different from the gentrified bronze cattle and horse sculptures that decorated Dallas's downtown across the Trinity River to the north.

David knew that most Latino blue-collar families liked garden styles that could be labeled as colorful and disorganized, from American and Mexican flags in flower beds exploding with high weeds to decorative pink flamingos and gray geese made from clay, plaster, or plastic and waterless fountains, all of which contributed to a chaotic, vibrant style that suited David's eclectic, passionate side.

David approached the code officer, who, upon seeing him, immediately stopped scribbling on his pad. David didn't introduce himself because there was no need to. Everyone in code enforcement knew who David Levin was.

David started by acknowledging the Latino man, Pedro Jimenez. "Hello, Pedro. Good to see you." He then turned toward the code officer. "So, what's the problem, Officer?"

"Mr. Jimenez here is arguing that his weeds aren't obnoxious vegetation."

David turned to Pedro and asked, "What kind of plants are they?"

"They're *yerbas*, Señor Levin, and we use these plants for medicine." He patted his stomach, adding, "We make teas for the stomach."

David stared at the officer. "I've known Mr. Jimenez for a long time. He's originally from Mexico. Given the Mexicans' ancient knowledge of this region, they don't distinguish between yerbas and the plants that the city wants."

The enforcer frowned. "I'm just enforcing code, sir."

He shook his head. "The city's use of the word *weed* for any plant that the city doesn't consider civilized is wrong."

"Weeds that are more than ten inches high are against code."

David continued. "Wildflowers, for instance, aren't invasive and noxious. They belong to our ecosystem. Many of our neighbors are growing all kinds of plants that are higher than ten inches—for instance, roses. So explain to me the difference between a rosebush and the medicinal plants that Mr. Jimenez is growing."

"Many yerbas are medicine," Pedro explained again. "It is *menta* … mint, good for the stomach."

The code official rolled his eyes. "Sir, you can take this to the municipal judge."

"Yes, I can," David countered, "but you're the beginning of the problem."

"I'm just enforcing the law, sir."

"No, the citation begins with you."

"The regulations have to be obeyed."

"The regulations just mention the word *weed*. You're harassing these people."

"As I said, I'm just enforcing the law."

Again, David shook his head. "See here. You have to understand Pedro's point."

"I understand his point, sir."

"No, you don't." He pointed toward the parking lot next to Firehouse 15. "Do you see any houses over there?"

The official glanced sideways. "It's a parking lot, sir."

"The lot was the location of two houses."

The officer didn't answer.

"One of those houses was used as a Protestant mission in the 1980s."

"Yes, sir."

"It was a church for the Latino community."

"Yes, sir."

"Do you know why that house is gone?"

"No."

"Because the church didn't know how to communicate with that community."

The official remained silent.

"The church insisted that the Latinos play the organ."

"I don't understand, sir. What's wrong with the organ?"

He added, "The whites wanted country folks from Mexico and Central Americans to play German High Church music when, instead, they wanted guitars and maracas. So, instead of just preaching the message, the whites focused on the wrong thing. They didn't let people be people. They wanted to turn these people into northern Europeans."

"Sorry about what happened to your church."

He shook his head. "It wasn't my church."

The code enforcer said nothing.

"All these people want is to be a part of this country, son," David said.

He frowned.

"Don't punish them for being different."

The officer growled, "We're not doing that."

"Just like the church, you're trying to turn them into something they're not."

"This isn't about race."

"True. It's about culture—my point exactly. You want everyone in this neighborhood to play the organ with their yards, and, son, you have to admit that one instrument is very boring. You need to speak to them and learn from them. Tell that to your supervisor in code enforcement."

Pedro stepped in. "I'll take care of the problem, Mr. Levin."

"Do you know what to do?" David asked him.

Pedro nodded.

David didn't give up. "Let plants be plants," he said, reminding himself of the transient nature of this community, as his father, a lawyer, often said when he reminisced about the Jewish settlers and former African American slaves who built it.

He turned around to renew his run and headed for a historic residential neighborhood of carefully crafted bungalows and prairie homes under canopied trees that offered him some of the shade he needed. The area was known as Winnetka Heights.

Once on Tyler Street, he turned south, and as soon as he reached Twelfth Street, he headed east, thinking of the soul power in a bowl of delicious black-eyed peas. The peas seductively smiled at him, nothing like the code officer's bad attitude or the crafty glares of the city's Landmark Commission officials a few months earlier.

Grilled about his application for a historic plaque for his Victorian building, his simple description of the house as a limestone structure wasn't meticulous because it was also a frame building. They had given him a very difficult time about this omission. In fact, most of the interior was built out of wood, including its wall panels, stairs, and upper hardwood floors. A wrap-around porch with gingerbread trim, floors, and fluted columns was made of wood but for the exterior limestone bricks that made up the walls of the first floor.

But he wasn't an architect. He hated asking the city for anything for himself, but he went to the meeting and tried to clarify things. "The outside is limestone," he said, irritated that he had to justify himself when his instincts told him that they were on the side of large development companies. These developers were always lurking around his precious neighborhood, ready to turn it into a new, antiseptic, and weedless version of Dallas. A historic building would dampen their secret agendas. He should have foreseen that ambush.

He was tired of the manipulation and control, like the constant fumes shot by jets over the skies of Dallas that, some said, were chemical agents to manipulate the weather or, worse, to control people. The allegations were serious. The fumes' metal composition, including aluminum and copper oxide particles, were associated with a microscopic technology connected with a new illness associated with itching, lesions, blue or red fibers that grew out of the skin, and rising neural disorders. He didn't know what was happening, except that this control mind-set reminded him of Hitler's euthanasia program that first targeted the mentally ill and the elderly, all in the name of ridding society of unwanted elements. Then, Hitler focused on other unwanted social groups, and the railroad cars filled with silent, unconscious victims came. Then, the gas chambers came. David knew he didn't have any answers, but he wasn't unconscious.

"People who don't know they're being attacked don't fight back," he said to himself. He had to insist on answers about what was being dumped on his head, the air, the water, and the land.

But he decided not to involve himself with his own conspiracy theories right then. He would pursue that later. Instead, he thought about his recent exchange with the city bureaucrats: "If the limestone of my house dates back to 1888, then my house is a historic landmark. Who cares about the wood?"

"The interior has been modified several times," the official said to him. "We have to ensure that the historical integrity has been preserved."

He frowned. "Interior toilets, for instance. What's wrong with toilets?" He tapped his fingers on the table, wondering what insanity had possessed him to apply for a historic plaque.

He was reminded of that moment when he had limped around a corner and turned north toward the stone stairs that took him up to the front door of his house. Generations of previous owners had eventually deeded a pale, peeling, uninviting house to his father back in the early 1960s. It was an affordable purchase due to its almost folksy, rundown, but still functional condition. Also, it was a house that could be furnished with inexpensive pieces and easy-to-replace rugs, appropriate for the blue-collar immigrants who walked in, muddy boots and all, to see his father, a pioneer in immigration law when no written regulations existed except for the Immigration and Nationality Act of 1952 and deportation proceedings were presided over by the very people who were deporting his clients, border patrol agents.

David remembered those days. The system became more consistent with people's constitutional rights when he joined his father's law firm. Today, however, the system was much more complicated and politically explosive, a corporate beast of sorts and the reason he bristled when asked, "What kind of law do you practice?" His best answer was, "Human," in order to avoid explaining something that often invited a negative response. Immigrants were the most reviled group in a country with a foundation made up of the same.

Still, he loved his profession. The natural disorder of this world brought out the best in him. No other attorney in the region rivaled him. So, with this thought, his damp hand pushed the front door until he found himself standing on old parquet floors in the foyer and facing a waiting area on the right.

CHAPTER 10

BLACK-EYED PEAS

To David's surprise, Gloria was picking up the mail from the receptionist's desk. He asked, "When did you get here?"

"Twenty minutes ago."

"Where's the receptionist?"

"Picking up a record at the courthouse," she replied.

"Everyone else?"

"Upstairs." She was referring to Jonathan, another attorney, and two paralegals.

Her office was behind the library, a good place to watch any hallway traffic coming in through the front and back doors. She served as his managing partner even though her share was only 10 percent of his professional corporation.

"I'll take a shower," David said, referring to the historically inappropriate amenity that his private office offered. "Meet me in the kitchen in fifteen minutes. I need lunch before discussing Isabel's case."

"Yes, Mr. Levin," she answered, surrendering to his penchant for clear instructions. "Mmm," she said, "what are you preparing today?"

"Black-eyed peas," he said, limping up the stairs.

"It's not New Year's."

"I need some soul power," he answered, relishing that he was defending his social group, just in case, not that he needed to do that with Gloria. "Need some Texas black-eyed peas," he added, half-irritated as he disappeared into his office. When he emerged from it, he was dressed in his summer uniform—a white, short-sleeved shirt and khaki pants.

The back of the house included a bathroom between Gloria's command center and two supply rooms adjacent to the kitchen. The kitchen faced the parking lot for employees.

Renovations over the years had replaced the wood-burning stove, the larder, and the scullery with a stovetop, a refrigerator, and a dishwasher/sink, in that order. Apart from these appliances and a microwave, along with the long marble countertop and butler sink, the remaining amenities, such as the wooden cabinets and open cupboards, offered a vintage look with a kitchen table in the center, authentic for the period in which the house was built. Traditional moldings around the windows along with tile backsplashes reinforced the Victorian atmosphere.

Inspecting the kitchen triggered more reminders of the meeting with the city Landmark people. It was practically impossible not to compromise the old architecture, he thought, even though he suspected that the animosity toward him also stemmed from his reputation as a troublemaker.

He limped around the table and opened the refrigerator.

Gloria strode in. She didn't raise the subject of Isabel Condorcanqui. She waited for him to do it after eating his black-eyed peas.

He glanced at her. "Who's answering the phones?"

She grinned. "The machine." She knew more about him than anyone else except his only child, Leah. After more than a decade with the FBI, Leah was a high-ranking member of the agency in Washington DC who checked on her high-strung, widowed father about three or four times a week via e-mails and phone calls. But these efforts couldn't be compared to Gloria's assistance. She made sure that his home was cleaned and stocked appropriately by delegating these tasks to the receptionist and paralegals and, occasionally, to Jonathan, who didn't have any objection to the multitasking, Renaissance style of this law firm. One day, he acted as a lawyer. The next day, he served as grocery shopper while Gloria acted as head receptionist.

David pulled a garlic head, a white onion, and a plump red tomato from a crisper drawer.

"I told Jonathan that you were going to cook," she said, "so he took the paralegals out to lunch."

"They don't want my black-eyed peas?" He pounded a handful of garlic cloves with a hammer that he had pulled out from under the sink.

Gloria served herself a cup of black coffee from the machine on the counter and sat down at the table and watched him. "You could use the meat tenderizer or the rolling pin. They're sanitized."

"A hammer is a man's tool," he grumbled.

She frowned. "The garlic and the onions stink up the entire house. Not everyone likes the smell, even a few clients."

"Burn some of your sage."

"You know that some people mistake it for marijuana."

He silently limped toward the gas stovetop and placed a saucepan on a burner, adding olive oil along with the condiments. Within minutes, the smell of garlic and onions invaded the room.

"Your knees are wearing out, Mr. Levin. You need to slow down," she said, expecting a crisp, impatient answer.

On the contrary, he turned his head and calmly said, "You're right. I'll reduce it to three times a week." He poured two cans of black-eyed peas, no salt added, into the saucepan. He covered the pan, filled his favorite mug with coffee, and sat down opposite her.

"No salt?" she asked, startled by the no-salt diet.

"Salt and black and red pepper will be mixed in—don't worry."

CHAPTER 11

THE LAW FAMILY

Gloria was an ideal fit for David's restless personality. Her demeanor could be described as implacable, and not subject to hasty judgments, although she could be opinionated, which was the reason he trusted her reproaches. One side of her challenged David's protocol of supervising everything, including the kitchen, but she also honored his self-discipline and high principles.

David's active mind constantly reminded her that bigotry was the greatest enemy of humanity. His favorite quote was Oliver Wendell Holmes Sr.'s famous description, "The mind of a bigot is like the pupil of the eye. The more light you pour into it, the more it will contract."

She appreciated his knowledge, the constant flow of information that coincided, reinforced, and sometimes challenged her values. Bigotry, for instance, was a condition that had plagued her childhood in Magdalena, New Mexico, where she was born. Her father had died when she was ten years old, so he couldn't protect her when she was ostracized by the Anglo community because she was half Navajo, or Diné. She was raised by her Navajo mother, who sometimes couldn't protect her when some Navajo looked down on her because of her Anglo heritage.

So she married a Mexican-born man, Juan García, who moved her to Dallas, as if destiny had carved out a direct road to David's law office. She had just turned twenty-five years old when David hired her as his receptionist. She gravitated naturally to David, and he to her. David respected her as Navajo and, more appropriately, as Dolii—or Bluebird, the master builder—because she was free to create good medicine while she grew into a legal professional. David allowed her to perform spiritual medicine rites with her drum and prayers to Father Sky and Mother Earth as she looked in the direction of her ancestors on Huerfano Mountain in New Mexico. That was her task. A master builder was necessary in every family.

Below the Diné Pride sign on the wall near her desk stood a two-foot-tall plaster statue of the Virgin of Guadalupe, an icon of the faith she had adopted when she married Juan, who never insisted that she abandon her traditional ways. On the contrary, he supported them.

The virgin's other name was Tonantzin, the Aztecs' Mother Earth, Honored Grandmother, Mother of Corn, and Bringer of Maize, consistent with the Diné's conversation of offering corn kernels grounded into corn cakes to ShimáNahasdzáán. Parallels abounded, and Juan had no problem understanding them, including the Navajo matrilineal and matriarchal culture or the painful memories of missionaries dragging Diné children to Christian schools where they were indoctrinated into the male-dominated ways of European civilization and religion.

Juan García, himself of indigenous blood—although diluted with Spanish genes—often talked about Tonantzin's sacred place on Tepeyac Hill, which had been burnt to the ground by Spanish priests and then replaced with the Virgin of Guadalupe. To Juan, the Virgin was Tonantzin. To Gloria, Tonantzin was ShimáNahasdzáán.

After Juan died, David became a more important part of Gloria's life. Both carved out an environment of a tightly knit, tolerant family of committed workers with intellectual and spiritual gifts. David's Hebrew prayers could often be heard from his office while Gloria drummed downstairs or outside, and the rest of the staff, who were Methodist, Baptist, and Roman Catholic, continued their daily tasks.

*****

When David's black-eyed peas reached a boiling point, he tasted a spoonful, turned down the heat, and glanced at Gloria, waving the spoon in the air. "Want to try some?"

She shook her head. "Ate a sandwich while you were jogging."

"Not in the mood, or you just don't like them?"

"My father made black-eyed peas every New Year's Eve."

David knew a lot about her family but had never heard the details of how her father had died, so he asked. "You've always told me that your father died in an accident. I assumed that it was a car accident. Care to tell me what happened?"

"He fell off a horse," she answered.

"Your father was a Texan, and Texans never fall off their horses!"

"Well," she said apologetically, "he did."

"Something must have happened. Did he get shot?"

"No. He was going up a mountain trail, and something scared the horse."

"For heaven's sake, Gloria, your father didn't fall off the horse. He was *thrown* off the horse!"

She arched her shoulders. "That's the way my mother describes it, maybe because evil spirits live in those high rocks, and my father didn't believe in those things. She probably tells the story that way in order to say that he wasn't aware of things."

"Well, tell the story correctly. It's humiliating to a Texan to fall off a horse. I don't care if he doesn't know how to ride one, though your father sounds like he did. Otherwise, he wouldn't have tackled that mountain trail."

"Do you know how to ride a horse?"

David bristled. "No, not really, but you'll never see me falling off one!" He proceeded to serve himself a bowl of peas and started lobbying for them. "Did you know that they were first cultivated in West Africa?"

"Hmm."

He consumed the peas as rapidly as he could. "This is a very nutritious, drought-tolerant legume, high in calcium content, which is why it's part of my menu. My knee joints need the calcium."

She glanced at her wristwatch. "It's one o'clock," she said, aware that she was about to hear one of his cultural lectures.

He paid no mind to the distraction and added, "The southern Christian tradition of eating them for prosperity on New Year's Eve started after the American Revolution, but the Jewish practice of eating them at Rosh Hashanah began a lot earlier."

She decided to be polite and asked, "When?"

"Over one thousand years ago."

She remained silent.

He rose from the chair and served himself more peas, adding, "These peas are consumed all over the world—in South America, the Middle East, Asia, Europe ..." He glanced through the window facing the parking lot. He saw Jonathan and the paralegals rushing back from lunch. They headed toward the front door, carefully avoiding the kitchen. The receptionist had not returned.

David limped back to the table and hovered over another bowl laced with garlic while Gloria settled into drinking coffee, oblivious to the growing bustle in the rest of the house. She patiently waited for him to eat all of his black-eyed peas before discussing Isabel's case.

Chapter 12

CHASING PORCUPINE

David first asked for details about Gloria's meeting with Isabel's physician. She replied, "Dr. Warner is her name, Elizabeth Warner. Dr. Warner uses hypnosis in order to avoid sedating the patient. She confirmed that after two sessions with Isabel, she appears to be telling the truth."

"So what exactly happened when you met Isabel?"

"Dr. Warner was on the floor when the nurses alerted her that I needed to speak with her. Isabel was having one of her episodes when I arrived and slammed a metal stool against a window, but then she calmed down. Dr. Warner will be instrumental in getting Isabel released without a bond by delivering a psychiatric opinion that Isabel isn't a danger to the community or a high flight risk."

Gloria's racehorse instinct to immediately jump into a theory, especially when unsure of the facts, forced David to stay focused. "Is Isabel credible?" he insisted.

"I think so. Dr. Warner's report will help. Why do you ask?"

"Because we may be chasing porcupine."

She stared at him.

In the silence that followed, she secretly amused herself at the mention of porcupine and rose from the chair to refill her cup. She sat down again. David was referring to a Native American story about a young girl who chased a porcupine up a tree. There were different versions, and David had his. According to his, the girl didn't care that porcupine could harm her, and she certainly wasn't measuring the distance off the ground in case she fell down. Her friends yelled and yelled that she shouldn't chase the porcupine blindly, but she didn't listen to them. She continued climbing, and when she reached the top of the tree and caught up with the porcupine, the tree began growing until it touched the door of heaven, where she and the porcupine disappeared.

"What are you trying to tell me?"

He grinned. "It's dangerous to just depend on Dr. Warner's opinion."

"Who's the porcupine?"

"Isabel Condorcanqui," he answered. "The madness starts with her."

She pushed the coffee cup away from her.

"Some Native Americans attach porcupine quills to their knife sheaths and shields because the quills are protective medicine," he offered. "They are the quills of knowledge."

"They don't attack with their quills, do they?" Gloria argued. "What's the danger, then?"

He responded, "The animal is protecting itself, so we have to make the right decisions." He waited a few seconds before adding, "How can we know that she's the real Isabel Condorcanqui?"

"Why would she impersonate Isabel?"

"I don't know," he answered with a shrug.

"She was carrying a school identification card when she was kidnapped."

"That doesn't explain how her handlers obtained her birth certificate."

"Unless they were part of the government," Gloria answered. "Certified birth certificates aren't issued to just anyone."

He nodded. "The only one who can confirm it is Antonio Condorcanqui."

"Yes, and a DNA test."

"How long did you speak with her?" he asked.

"More than two hours, almost three."

"Enough to form an initial assessment. What do you think is behind what she said?"

"She said a lot. I don't think she's an impostor."

"You know the government may not buy her story."

She nodded.

"The story about chasing porcupine is about making the right choices."

"I know." Gloria too had been forced to make a few important decisions. Soon after her husband had died, David had offered to pay for a law school education at a private university in Dallas. By then, her children were older, so she had accepted the offer in spite of her fears that she wouldn't make it through law school. But she did. When she graduated, she began to work for David as an attorney.

"For example, my people have the Exodus. Just like that girl chasing porcupine, they had to follow Moses but weren't completely convinced about it. Moses had to work hard to convince everyone. He did. Once they reached the other side of the Red Sea, they didn't obey him. Do you know why?"

She shook her head.

"After centuries of servitude, they couldn't transform themselves into a freed people."

"So, the tree didn't join heaven," she said.

"Chasing porcupine," he answered, "represents the act of taking responsibility for your own life, of making the correct decision. My people didn't want to chase porcupine. They didn't want to take the risk. They wanted to continue living as victims. So, God left them in the desert for forty years until they got it. It took forty years to get rid of that generation. They were promised the Promised Land, but they never understood that it was about making a choice, like pursuing their personal liberation."

"If Isabel is the madness, what should we do?"

"The madness," he said, "begins with her because she can't decide what she is. We have to be mindful of what she's doing because, after all, her story is that they killed Pachamama."

"So, she's dead."

"She went through a moral and spiritual death, yes. But she's still alive. She needs a lot of help. Victims are only interested in their victimization."

"I don't understand."

"Isabel has crossed the Red Sea. She has to decide who she wants to be. She spent forty years in bondage. She had many opportunities to get away from her captors, but she didn't do that. So, right now, she has to move on. We have to help her move on because she will try to self-sabotage. That's what victims do. They're more interested in their stories than living life to the fullest. God leaves victims in the desert. But you and I have been given this opportunity to help her."

"We can include Dr. Warner's opinion at the hearing."

"They may forgo a bond hearing."

"Should I ask for a bond hearing?"

He shook his head. "Ask them to release her on her own personal recognizance. You may get it with Karl Segal's help."

"I recorded most of our conversation," Gloria offered.

"I'll listen to it upstairs."

"In any event," Gloria added, "Isabel's a descendant of the leader of one of the most powerful indigenous rebellions of Perú. It happened in 1780, but it's not ancient history to many Peruvians."

David nodded. "There's an ulterior reason why Karl asked me if I would take this case. I don't believe the head federal prosecutor of human trafficking cases is acting without a hidden agenda. This is outside the box."

"But he's a good friend of yours," she said.

"He's a prosecutor, Gloria. He functions in a world that isn't transparent."

"That's harsh, don't you think?"

"Don't take anything for granted." His phone conversation with Karl days ago flashed through his mind.

As soon as he took the call, Karl's voice pressed through the receiver. "Figuring this one out is your specialty," Karl had said, "although there are a few telltale signs that Isabel is plugged into the trafficking cartel of Perú with ties to Colombia, Spain, and Mexico, maybe a double life."

Karl had built a different scenario about Antonio. In fact, Karl wasn't certain that Isabel had a brother, but, if she did, his probable name was Antonio Condorcanqui and he was sourcing articles about the human-trafficking cartels connected with top-tier officials of several governments.

"I'll look for those articles," David had said.

Karl responded, "Confessions of a Revolutionary." The informant was Antonio, alias El Condor. "The journalist is Rafael Aguilar," Karl added, "a freelance writer from Venta Prieta, Hidalgo, Mexico."

"I know about Venta Prieta."

"You do?" Karl asked.

"You know how much genealogical research I do, and I've researched that community. There's a Mexican-Indian-Jewish enclave there."

"Why would Aguilar be interested in helping a Peruvian revolutionary?"

"Why not? Persecution resonates with these Mexican Indian Jews, whose ancestors fled the Spanish Inquisition by moving into remote parts of Mexico. They maintained clandestine rites known as Secret Saturday, or Sábado Secreto. A few of his ancestors didn't survive official burnings in Spain."

"Sephardic Jews?"

"Enclaves survived in and around Pachuca, Hidalgo, an important mining center during Spanish colonial rule. Venta Prieta is nearby. It was part of the silver road."

Karl patiently waited for David to finish his analysis of the Sephardic Jews of Mexico. David added, "Some called them Crypto-Jews because of their forced conversion to Roman Catholicism while they kept clandestine synagogues or home-based informal rites. Some relocated to Mexico City. However, when their persecution intensified there, they moved to places like Pachuca, fifty-five miles to the northeast of Mexico City."

Karl continued. "Isabel needs a good lawyer, someone who'll stand up for her. She'll smell you and figure you out. She may give us leads to Antonio."

David laughed. "Why would she help with Antonio?"

"Antonio Condorcanqui has valuable information about the slave trade."

"Why don't you contact Antonio or Rafael Aguilar? Propose a deal?"

"That's a possibility. However, this is an opportunity to connect through someone in Antonio's family." After Karl rattled off more details about Isabel's arrest, whereabouts, and possible options for her release, he said that he would fax documents that David could submit to him under the Freedom of Information Act.

David nodded to himself, closing with, "I'll send Gloria to interview Isabel."

"Are you sure Gloria is up to it?"

"Both are Indians. They're familiar with persecution. Something will resonate."

*****

Gloria's voice brought David back to the present. "Her direct ancestor's name was Juan Bautista Condorcanqui, hence her surname, the half-brother of the man who led the rebellion."

"According to her birth certificate, her second name is Pacha. What did she say about that?"

"That her mother is a descendant of the mother of Atahualpa."

David leaned against the table. "Are we supposed to drown the government with hundreds of years of history?"

"Indians have a different way of looking at the ancestors, Mr. Levin."

He sat back. "That expert testimony will be challenged. We need to bolster it with more opinions. Of course, they're just opinions."

Gloria blinked and added, "We have to look at these events as the systematic extermination of that family, which is why she and her brother, Antonio, were kidnapped. Some important people have followed a campaign to get rid of the descendants of the royal Inca."

He remained silent.

"It's a good argument," she insisted. "You can rely on the recording. Antonio was fourteen. Both were children. Under international law, the kidnapping of children is genocide. Children are still being abducted in order to systematically control native Andeans."

He relented. "You mentioned Juan Bautista. What happened to him?"

"He was exiled to Spain after the execution of José Gabriel."

"Where?"

"Ceuta."

"Same place that Isabel was transferred to?"

She nodded. "Juan Bautista spent forty years in exile in Ceuta."

"And Isabel has spent forty years in exile. Interesting coincidence."

Again, she nodded, adding, "If so, don't we have to ask ourselves who's masterminding this? I'm beginning to think that they aren't coincidences. When Juan Bautista came back through Buenos Aires, Isabel says that Simón Bolívar kept him away from Perú. By then, he was an old man of eighty-six years."

"What's the evidence?"

"A letter he wrote to Bolívar. Bolívar never wrote back."

"Maybe his answer was lost in the mail. Wasn't he fighting the Spanish?"

"Yes. However, she says that Bolívar was probably anti-Inca."

He nodded. "Maybe he wasn't anti-Inca but anti-establishment because the Peruvian establishment was anti-Inca."

"Again, it's part of her story."

"The coffeepot still has coffee. Have more," he offered with a smile.

"I've had enough, Mr. Levin."

Meanwhile, he walked to the refrigerator and pulled out two plastic bottles of water. His office was recycling the bottles. "I'm going upstairs to listen to your recording."

CHAPTER 13

THEY KILLED PACHAMAMA

When David assigned the case to Gloria, he didn't mention all of Karl's comments—for instance, the interest in Antonio Condorcanqui—because they were meant for him. He was the senior attorney. Hidden under piles of papers on his desk were additional narratives that he kept for himself.

Isabel's arrest in the kitchen of the main house while she bled profusely had turned the arrest into a rescue mission that led to the city's public hospital. David wondered when it was that ICE had found the opportunity to process her in view of what had transpired, and, indeed, pieces of the story showed up afterward, although not the whole picture.

Within six hours of his black-eyed peas lunch, he walked down the hallway downstairs and peered through Gloria's open door. He was prepared for one of their high-level conversations that never included the rest of the staff. She was looking down at the screen of her laptop. She glanced up and smiled. She asked, "Did you listen to all of the recording?"

"May I come in?" he asked.

"Of course." She pushed down the lid of the laptop and waited for him to take a seat in front of her desk.

"Yes, I did," he answered.

"So, what do you think?"

He wasn't one to jump to conclusions, but by his own admission Isabel had triggered many issues. He wanted to take a philosophical approach. "Joseph Campbell has something to say about this."

She nodded even though she had never had any spare time to read Joseph Campbell. She had to finish raising three children into adulthood when her husband died six years earlier. Then she started law school a year later, and now she was learning how to be a real lawyer. David's encyclopedic knowledge always preceded the point he wanted to make. She listened.

"As you know, he was a great teacher and writer on comparative mythology," he said even though she had heard this many times over the years, "who wrote that the spell of the past is being destroyed while mankind comes to maturity."

She waited.

"For instance, let's consider why we got involved in this case. No place is safe unless we make it safe."

"I ... I don't understand."

"She's an Indian, like you."

"She's persecuted. What's new?"

"They killed Pachamama," he added.

"Duly noted. However, I'm not familiar with Pachamama. I just know that she's an Andean deity."

He grinned. "She's Mother World, also Mother Earth, to the indigenous people of the Andes. She's the heart. What the record doesn't show is that Isabel *is* Pachamama."

"Why?"

"Isabel has three important names—Condorcanqui, Pacha, and Túpac Amaru—associated with the sacred symbols of the condor—pacha, for world, and Amaru, for cosmic snake. You can't ignore the meaning of these symbols, and they come together with her. However, it's difficult to show persecution due to membership in that particular social group because the thread to the Inca's royal family has been officially destroyed. Nevertheless, her family group is unique."

"So you're agreeing with the argument of systematic extermination?"

"Damn right. It's persecution of a mythological conversation, but it transcends into a genetic line that goes back to their creation. It's a bombshell to the status quo because the status quo destroyed the Inca."

She considered that. "So they kidnapped her."

"Think about it, Gloria. She's part of the monarchical identity of the Andean region. In addition, the condor is the national bird of six countries: Argentina, Bolivia, Chile, Colombia, Ecuador, and Perú—six countries, one identity."

"Spain is a monarchy too."

"The Spanish understand the concept of the divine right of kings and queens, although it's diluted with democratic principles. The Spanish know that these queens and kings give the country an identity, a point of unification."

"I still believe it's bizarre that we're dealing with this in these times.'"

"When it gets to the point of kidnapping people and placing them in the slave trade, it's extreme, but it still goes on in other ways. Thousands of disappearances were taking place in those days—for example, in Chile and Argentina. Those governments were targeting potential subversives."

"Even Indians?"

"Yes, especially Indians. Any resistance to domination by certain groups."

"If they kept her off the radar for so long, what is she doing here?"

"There's an ulterior motive to bringing her to the United States. They were going to take her to Victor, Colorado. There's a lot of mining over there. We don't know anything yet. Karl mentioned her brother, who has been generating articles about the slave trade in Perú's mining communities."

"You didn't tell me that, Mr. Levin."

"Didn't want to confuse things."

"How should we play this?"

"We're going to let that play itself out. Right now, even though I'm interested in Antonio Condorcanqui, we can't lose sight of our obligation to defend Isabel. We have to connect the threads of what happened forty years ago to today."

"As you like to say, the whole thing is being worked out on another level."

He added, "We also have to keep things simple, Gloria. If we talk about group persecution because she's a Quechua of royal descent, we won't get anywhere. But if we pursue a more practical approach that our government officials can understand, then we have a chance at some good, solid relief. The government understands the concept of family. It's feasible that important people in Perú are persecuting her because of her family line and its association with three important mythological names."

She nodded.

"By the way," David added, "I have a few extra documents that I didn't give you."

"I know," she answered.

"So, tell me, when was she taken to the ICE intake office?"

Gloria drew a deep breath. "An ambulance took her to the emergency room immediately after her arrest. They called Dr. Warner, who wanted to keep her under observation. However, once the ER took care of the injuries, she was transferred to the ICE intake facility, where she was coded as a low security risk but segregated for a few hours, enough time for them to be concerned about her mental state. Her allegations against top-tier officials in the Colombian and Peruvian governments prompted the call to Karl Segal. He approved her transfer back to Dr. Warner's care. By then, ICE had an alien file, which Karl delivered to you."

"Isabel sounded less distressed when she spoke with you," David mentioned.

"Dr. Warner told me that self-injuries like Isabel's are a result of guilt, rage, self-hate, previous trauma, a way to control one's life—nothing to do with insanity. She's the typical victim of slave trafficking. She talked herself into being a part of those families she worked for. It's an adaptive mechanism that Dr. Warner calls battered person syndrome. She says that Isabel needs an inner circle of friends who can stay objective."

"Interesting."

"So, am I still chasing porcupine?"

He laughed.

"Where do I start? Isabel will be released in a few days from the hospital to an ICE detention center."

"Prepare for her release on her own recognizance."

"I doubt it."

"Then negotiate for a low bond," David said.

"Who will pay for it?"

"We will."

She almost choked. "Mr. Levin, I don't have the money."

"You're a partner in this law firm. We will both share it."

"But what if it's too high?"

"Then you're not being a real lawyer."

"You're putting me in a terrible position."

"Why?"

"I can't take personal responsibility for a woman I don't know."

"If you don't believe her, then no one will. You want to keep her company in the desert?"

"The government will require a high bond."

"Have they implied that?"

She shook her head.

"Then, make an appointment with Karl. Negotiate with him. He wants her brother, Antonio Condorcanqui. You need to go home." He stood up.

"I have two hearings to prepare for."

He said anyway, "Call Karl tomorrow morning. He's waiting for our next move."

"Should I use Dr. Warner for the bond hearing?"

He frowned. "Stop jumping on the horse. Speak with Karl first. Determine what boundaries he wants. In the meantime, find a cultural or historical anthropologist on Perú who can help us with Pachamama."

She nodded.

"Enter the mystery without fretting, Gloria. We need to prove the chronology of changes in Perú without losing the thread of past and current persecution against Isabel's family, whether they're Inca, Quechua, or Condorcanqui. Isabel is unable to avail herself of the protection of her native country. They killed her soul forty years ago. Also, follow up on the issue of resettlement because the government will definitely try to send her to Spain."

"I don't think it's that serious."

"Stay neutral. You've been trained to be a critical thinker. Don't believe anything, but, at the same time, believe everything."

CHAPTER 14

SANTA MARTA

Antonio's eyes raced left and right, watching the downtown crowd around the fountain in front of the Casa de la Aduana that first belonged to Joaquin de Mier, the Spaniard who had received a very ill Bolívar. The two-story, balconied, whitewashed house faced two rows of parked mini-taxicabs whose bright yellow competed for Antonio's attention. He didn't know if his instincts that he was being followed were correct, but the unease was there when he slipped through the crowd. Faces turned to him, though most of the eyes were unfocused. It was a sign that they, like he, were waging a battle against the oppressive heat of Santa Marta.

The humidity wasn't as bad as Cartagena's, though. In addition, a faint sea breeze wafted in through the main plaza, but Antonio paid no mind to it because he was trying to steal a glimpse of the historian in the small plaza adjacent to the Casa de la Aduana. The crowd and the taxicabs and the trees made that difficult. Somewhat irritated, he headed toward the landmark and crossed the street, scurrying between pedestrians who jostled for some kind of space.

Swarms of students from all countries were assaulting the very place where he would continue his search for the Dominican priest. These students were the same people who quoted, "The past gets in the way of fully being present today," and were, in fact, the least likely to be in touch with the past, particularly *his* past. Pacha K'anchay was the light of the cosmos, not the Internet.

The city of Santa Marta was founded four years after Hernán Cortés began the destruction of Tenótchtitlan in Mexico. Unlike Cortés and city founder Rodrigo de Bastidas, who wanted to re-create Spain in the New World, Antonio was interested in finding what had survived of Bolívar's true legacy. Facts about Bolívar had a tendency to be erased, ignored, or lost, as was likely the case of Bolívar's response to Juan Bautista Condorcanqui and Bolívar's letter donating his heart to the people of Cuzco.

Antonio followed the Quechuan philosophy that treated interpersonal connections as components of a larger cosmological world in which one human being opened the way for another even though separated by great physical distances and times. Some of these threads were the implicit pathways that opened the door for Juan Bautista to communicate with Bolívar after forty years of exile. Juan Bautista was imprisoned in Cuzco nearly two months after Simón Bolívar was born. Then there was the fact that Juan Bautista arrived from Ceuta in Buenos Aires several months after Bolívar arrived in Quito, Ecuador, on June 16, 1822, to initiate his Andean war against Spain.

Antonio mulled over these connections while waiting in the plaza for the historian Dr. Miguel Baralt, as another topic began lurking in his head. By the time Bolívar boarded his ship, the *Manuel*, from Barranquilla to Santa Marta, he could hardly walk. His breathing was difficult, and his cough had worsened. Barely able to stand without assistance, he spoke in a hoarse voice, holding a handkerchief that absorbed his frequent tears. He was disheartened, isolated, banished, and very ill. By the time he arrived in Santa Marta, he was ready to die but strong enough to dictate his farewell letters and last will and testament ten days later.

Bolívar was aware that the five nations he liberated would coexist only as a result of his mere will while he was alive and that his mystical vision of a federation of nations couldn't be enforced by rules after he was gone. These five region-nations were multiple forms of an organized universe ruled by a European hierarchy whose inherent friction with local, living communities was controlled by force. Nonetheless, the theme of tyrant was overstated against Bolívar himself, and, as if to add salt to a festering wound, a weakening commitment to come together as a union of nations in one form or another brought on his spiritual death.

Rumors were that he was assassinated by agents sent by US president Andrew Jackson, who intercepted the *Manuel*, rumors that were met with a shrug in the Colombian academic community. Not that Jackson was a saint, but the rumor mill, according to most local historians like Dr. Baralt, was a noisy promoter of political agendas that continued the old divide-and-conquer paradigm to this day, distracting the public from facts that stood by their own merit.

Dr. Miguel Baralt, a member of the intellectual elite of the city, appeared a few minutes later. He was a short, bony man with the countenance of a scholar, a Beethoven-like mane of gray hair, large dark eyes, a clean-shaven face, and a raspy voice that spoke the very precise Spanish of a man from Bogotá.

Antonio shook his hand. Both settled into a slow stride toward the pedestrian walk along the waterfront of the bay. While they strolled, Antonio filled him in on everything that had happened until that point. "In Barranquilla, I went to the archdiocese. After inspecting the outside of the place, I decided to leave it to you to make the contact."

They stopped in front of the statue of Rodrigo de Bastidas. "So what do you have in mind?" Baralt asked. "Should we look for the Dominican priest?"

Antonio shrugged. "You tell me."

He grinned. "Well, the last time I checked, they told me that Father Arriaga was in Barranquilla."

"When?"

"I received this information a week ago. Curia Arzobispal," he answered. "He's getting ready to leave for Spain."

"Why didn't you call him?"

"I must confess that I wanted to gather more information before speaking to him."

"What else is there to gather?" Antonio answered.

Baralt nodded. "No sense in visiting the cathedral here in Santa Marta. I tried that route."

"They're denying the existence of the letter?"

"The letter, my friend, is probably in an archive in the Vatican by now. That's what my contact said."

"So, they're not denying its existence?"

"True, but we can't rely on that."

"You know a lot about the historical record, Dr. Baralt. The historical archives reflect that Bolívar's heart was kept in a coffer of lead and silver and delivered to the bishop of Santa Marta when Bolívar died in 1830. No one disputes that Bolívar was buried in the aisle facing the altar of San José of the cathedral, but the coffer was separated from those remains."

"Yes. When an earthquake hit Santa Marta in 1834, his coffin was spit out from the ground, and that's when his remains were moved to the central aisle in front of the main altar. The inventory taken of his remains when they were given to Venezuela in 1842 mentions a receptacle containing his heart. By then, the heart was dust. The inventory duly notes that the coffer would remain in Colombia."

"The coffer lost its importance. It was empty."

"Yes, but up to a point," Baralt replied. "The coffer didn't lose its historical importance. The paper trail shows that the coffer was saved in 1860 during a fire. When a new cathedral was completed in 1868, the priest who returned the coffer to the bishop verified this in a letter. The receptacle was safeguarded near the sacristy. In 1980, the bishop then authorized an investigation, but it was stopped by another official of the church, who requested permission from the Vatican. The permission hasn't been issued."

"In addition, the letter was written on the same day that Bolívar dictated his farewell letter and last will and testament."

"Yes, December 10, 1830, so it's consistent with the circumstances."

"In the sixth clause of his last will and testament," Antonio reminded him, "he ordered the return of the medal that he received from the Congress of Bolivia as evidence of his true, undying affection for Bolivia. The gesture is unique because it's the only clause that mentions anything like this."

"Maybe because the country was named after him," Baralt ventured.

"Where is Father Arriaga now?"

"Probably still in Barranquilla. Father Arriaga is being evasive. He doesn't want to get in trouble with his superiors."

"How can he get in trouble when he made a copy of another copy?"

Dr. Baralt said, "He copied it without permission, my friend."

"Did you mention the copy to your contact?"

He shook his head.

"They're unaware of the copy?"

"I said nothing about the copy."

"He's the key, then."

He nodded.

"We should not waste any time. So, how do we contact him?"

Baralt grinned. "Some historical research. Barranquilla is just an hour and fifteen minutes away."

He nodded.

Baralt quipped, "I'll call and make an appointment for this afternoon," as he pulled out his phone. Seconds later, he was speaking with a historian who worked in the archdiocese's library. When he hung up, he pocketed the phone. "*Listo*, he'll see me at three o'clock today."

CHAPTER 15

HUNTER, MASTER BUILDER, AND WARRIOR

The sun was already melting the pavement of downtown Dallas when Gloria stepped down from the sidewalk and crossed the street toward the federal building. Two policemen on the northwest street corner of the building glanced at her superficially while a third officer, who guarded the main entrance, took a special interest. Maybe it was the way she walked. Maybe it was the energy she carried.

Early, before breakfast, she had done a sage offering and invoked the ancient spirit of the hunt of her people, whose ability was to see far beyond the horizon. The ancestors had worked hard to get her to this point in her life, and now, downtown's high, thick walls of concrete, glass, and steel required her to ignore the stifling heat and concentrate on her mission. She was a frequent visitor, always ferrying legal files in her arms. On this occasion, however, her load was lighter, with only Isabel's file and an appointment with Karl Segal in fifteen minutes.

The entrance was swarming with people trying to get in line in front of the security scanner. She glanced at her wristwatch. Time was moving fast.

After she recovered her belongings from the scanner, she took the elevator. Upon reaching Karl's floor, she stepped onto the green carpet and headed toward the double doors of the US Attorney's Office. The lobby was flanked by dark brown leather chairs and three table lamps on the right, and it opened into a conference room at the end.

She waited only a few minutes before Karl escorted her to his private office. Tall and trim, he wore a beard that was whiter than it had been when she last saw him years ago, when he had visited David's office. At that time, she worked as a paralegal. Her eyes inspected the photographs on the wall behind Karl's massive leather chair. Each had a personal autograph from one of the last five presidents of the United States, which spoke a lot about Karl's survival skills. The long gallery of attorneys general on the same wall resonated with the same message. Meanwhile, Karl wasted no time and shifted his attention from admiring her perfectly braided hair that fell over a navy blue suit to a file on his desk. He opened it. "Isabel Condorcanqui."

Her composure calm, she nodded.

He glanced up. "How is she doing?"

"She appears to be doing well in spite of her circumstances."

Karl wrinkled his forehead.

"What I've been able to gather," she said, "is that she was the cook of the group."

"Yes, eleven men plus two male handlers."

She added, "They tied her up and locked her in a small metal building behind the house at night in order to keep her away from the other men."

He thumbed through the file. "Looks like they were there for two months."

"Were all of them from Perú?" Gloria asked.

Karl shook his head. "Mexicans. They were smuggled from Mexico through Brownsville, Texas. That's how they reached south Dallas."

She had come to the same conclusion.

"Used back roads for the most part, which aren't watched as closely as the highways."

"Do you know how she landed in Mexico?"

His face tightened. "Yes," he said. "Thousands of people are trafficked into the United States each year. We don't know how many children. My guess is that the total number of victims is in the millions. They're brought in as enslaved domestics, forced prostitutes, or agricultural workers, to name the top occupations, run by transnational networks. Latin America, like Africa, offers a fertile ground for human trafficking given its high birth rate, poverty, and corruption, particularly among law enforcement officials. It's a deeply stratified society that doesn't offer reasonable access to capital or gender equality, not to mention the drug trade and its internal conflicts—all good sources of child soldiers, or terrorists and gangs."

"How many Peruvians are brought in?"

"A minority. Most are Chinese, Mexican, or Vietnamese." He glanced around, adding, "This is an international network."

"That also feeds the mining communities of South America," she said.

He nodded. "If the victims can't pay the smuggler, then the smuggler 'sells' them to the new employer, who charges them for rent, food, lodging, and protection in an arrangement known as debt bondage. Dehydration, hunger, fear, and mental and physical abuse are generally part of the package, as well."

"Are you going to prosecute her?" she asked.

Karl's eyes were fixed on her face. "We could do that for illegal entry, but she's a witness. I can recommend that she be paroled in as a witness. However, once we're finished with the prosecution of her handlers, I doubt that a judge will give her any relief."

"Anything is a lot better than facing a federal charge of illegal entry."

He remained silent.

She felt a chill seep into her. "Though anything is possible."

"What's possible?"

"Asylum."

"If she's credible. We still have no idea whether she's a smuggler or a victim. Judges don't like smugglers, even the victims of smuggling rings."

"This woman was abducted from Cuzco when she was seventeen years of age," Gloria countered.

He glanced down at the file. "According to *her.*"

"David is fond of quoting Leviticus …"

Karl interrupted, "You shall treat the stranger who sojourns with you as the native among you, and you shall love him as yourself, for you were aliens in the land of Egypt." He was aware that she was trying to appeal to his emotions. He grinned. "Good point. But you don't have a lot of time. She's been in the country for over two months. Preparing an asylum case before the one-year deadline isn't easy unless we conduct a credible fear interview right now."

"We're going to request asylum in any event."

"This woman resettled in Spain."

"She was a hostage."

He sat back in his swivel chair. "The parole will avoid a bond right now. However, if you're going to go for asylum, I can't buy you time."

"She can have a credible fear interview."

"But is she a smuggler or a victim?"

"David will decide this."

"She tried to commit suicide," he said.

"That doesn't establish anything."

"Maybe she did that because she's a smuggler. She was caught."

Gloria remained silent.

"If you opt for asylum, don't try to delay it."

"David said you're interested in her brother, Antonio Condorcanqui."

"Yes."

"Why, if you have doubts about her identity and motives?"

"I may have doubts, but I can't assume that she's not Isabel Condorcanqui or a victim. Her birth certificate is legitimate according to Peruvian authorities."

"So they've been alerted that she's in Dallas."

He nodded and asked, "Has Antonio been in touch with her?"

"No. First, the handlers told her that he was killed in Cuzco. When they approached her about coming to the United States, they told her that he was alive." Gloria omitted any mention about Colombia even though Karl was probably aware of Antonio's whereabouts.

"I just mentioned that law enforcement officials are often implicated in human smuggling networks," he said. "Antonio has information that will help us identify high government officials in Perú and Colombia connected with the slave trade in the United States."

"How will Antonio benefit my client?" she asked.

"He may prove that what happened to her forty years ago is still happening today. A lot could ride on this man."

"I don't understand."

He grinned. "Antonio worked for the Peruvian National Police. Before that, he was a member of the insurgent movement."

"Isabel said that she came to the United States because they promised her that they would help her find her brother."

"Who promised her that?"

"Her handlers in Spain."

Karl nodded. "And now he's sourcing articles that are damaging Isabel's handlers, hence their interest in him. It's likely that they're trying to use her as bait if she's the real deal." He thumbed through the file and glanced up. "If you prove that she has suffered substantial physical or mental abuse as a victim of the slave trade and she cooperates with us in the investigation or prosecution of these criminals, we can certify her for a special visa. We can do the same for Antonio Condorcanqui."

"The question is whether he'll be amenable to cooperating."

Karl shifted in his chair but said nothing.

She returned to the subject matter of Isabel's asylum claim. "Isabel said that she can't return to Perú because of her family's connection to the Inca."

"What's so special about that? The Inca aren't recognized as a social group."

She shook her head. "She's a Quechua and a descendant of the royal Inca family." She leaned over the edge of his desk. "Her primary ancestor was exiled because his brother, José Gabriel Condorcanqui, led a powerful indigenous rebellion against the Spanish."

"When did that take place?"

"In 1780."

He suppressed a grin, trying to take the information seriously. "That was centuries ago, Gloria."

"Yes, I know."

He was amused by her zeal. "This is a predictable world that doesn't give us a lot of choices."

"We can probably show a reasonable possibility that she's a member of a group being singled out for persecution by corrupt law enforcement officials who abducted and enslaved her."

"There are no recent events that support that," he argued.

"Perú continues to have a high incidence of disappearances. If there's no official record of these disappearances, that doesn't mean they didn't happen. For instance, in 2003, a Truth and Reconciliation Commission reached the conclusion that there were 69,280 murders from 1980 to 2000, most of which occurred in the region of Ayacucho. Most who disappeared were indigenous. They're still finding the mass graves."

"But were they politically motivated?"

"They were the by-product of an ideological internal conflict."

"Isabel and Antonio didn't live in Ayacucho."

"True, but Antonio joined the guerrilla movement."

Karl frowned. "That happened after they tried to kidnap him, of course, assuming that the kidnapping did happen. So, why is her ancient lineage important? She's been a part of the human trafficking world for forty years." He leaned against the back of his chair and pressed his index finger against his temple. "Those people are very smart. She's manipulating you."

She remained silent.

"She's drawing you into her black hole."

"I have very good instincts myself. Besides, why have you taken a special interest in this case?"

Karl didn't answer the question. Instead, he said, "The best person to guide you is David Levin. He'll figure something out."

"For instance?"

"First of all, I'll recommend her parole to the United States as a witness. In the meantime, tell David that I'm offering certification for a U visa for Isabel and Antonio if both help us with the investigation of those officials in Latin America."

"How can we do that if Isabel hasn't spoken with Antonio in forty years?"

"David will figure it out," he replied.

She stood up while thinking of Isabel's words to her: "Ayni isn't for sale." According to her research, *ayni* was the Andean word for the sacred law of reciprocity between humanity and the Other World and vice versa, and between human beings. The Navajo spirit of the hunt could see far and wide, and it would help her. She was hunter, master builder, and warrior.

*****

From his seat in the passenger side of the Renault, Antonio checked the street activity through the window. Nothing appeared out of place.

Dr. Baralt, who was behind the wheel, glanced at his wristwatch, mindful that he was early, but the extra time gave him the opportunity to make another call to the priest who worked for the archdiocese. Baralt had agreed not to reveal Antonio's real identity. By then, nothing should have pointed to Antonio's articles. They had stirred up passionate sermons against allegations that incriminated the Roman Catholic Church in the abduction and disappearances of children of so-called subversives in the Dirty War of Argentina.

He parked the Renault on the street across from the archdiocese's bookstore, Librería San Pablo, and waited, thus avoiding the main doors of the archdiocese's building. His car was a short distance from a white retaining wall that made way for a red tile staircase leading to those arched doors.

After both exited the car and crossed the smaller door down a corridor that divided the church on the right from a vestibule and garden on the left, Antonio inspected the visitors in the church through a row of glass windows, eyeing possible exit strategies. They opted to wait for Father Andrade in the garden. Minutes later, a thirty-something-year-old priest dressed in a white habit appeared through the front door, the same one they had used. The priest greeted Baralt. "*Doctor!*"

Both stood up. "Buenas tardes," Baralt replied, turning toward Antonio.

"This is Father Julio Andrade," he said with precision as Antonio extended his hand.

Father Andrade shook it.

Antonio noticed no unusual activity in his peripheral vision.

The priest smiled. "Dr. Baralt tells me that you're looking for someone who's been conducting some research of interest to you."

"Yes," Antonio responded. "Father Nestor Arriaga."

They followed the priest into an adjacent office. Andrade sat behind the desk, and Baralt and Antonio sat in front of him.

"And when did you meet him?"

"Actually, Dr. Baralt met him."

Baralt took the lead and followed their agreed strategy. "Father Arriaga mentioned a letter he had found in the archives of the cathedral in Santa Marta. It's a letter that was signed by Bolívar."

"And why is this letter so important?" Andrade asked.

They had decided to be direct. "Because Bolívar left instructions for his heart to be buried in Cuzco."

Father Andrade's face remained impassive. "Hmm. What happened to his heart?"

"It remains in the Cathedral of Santa Marta," Baralt answered. "No one has addressed the issue. We were directed to find Father Arriaga here."

Andrade frowned. "I don't know about this letter. Who told you that you could find him here?"

Baralt answered, "My contact in the Cathedral of Santa Marta."

"Have you ever spoken with him?" The tone of his voice had dropped the friendliness, but it remained polite.

"Yes. I met him many months ago," Baralt said. "We had a conversation about this letter, which he saw himself. We're only trying to ensure the historical accuracy of the letter before publishing an article about it."

Again, Andrade frowned. "I wouldn't do that," he mentioned.

Baralt smiled. "Why not? As a colleague, I want to do what is right. We need to be on the right side of history, if we can."

Father Andrade stood up. "Let me see what I can find. Are you returning to Santa Marta right now?"

Antonio interjected. "We'll be at the Prado Hotel tonight." He could feel sweat drops forming on his forehead. He pulled himself up after Andrade left and proceeded to leave through the front door with Baralt leading the way. An inclined driveway with a white electric gate stood behind the bookstore. As soon as they returned to the Renault, the gate opened and a gray Chevrolet Captiva drove out. Baralt immediately recognized the driver. Their plan had worked.

Baralt grinned. "Where do we go from here?"

"Just follow him, *hermano.*"

Baralt followed Father Arriaga to the parking lot of the Prado Hotel, where they intercepted him.

Arriaga recognized him. "How did you know?"

"We waited outside of the parking lot."

They shook hands.

Baralt added, "This is my friend Antonio."

Father Arriaga nodded. He was wearing civilian clothes. "I was getting ready to pack when Father Andrade alerted me. Allow me," he said, pulling a briefcase out of the backseat. He laughed nervously. "Security. Don't want to get careless."

Baralt and Antonio exchanged glances.

Antonio pointed toward the entrance of the historic hotel. "Why don't we go to the restaurant?"

Father Arriaga scratched his chin. "I'd rather go to a more private place." He pointed at his briefcase. "There is a document that I have to show you."

Again, Baralt and Antonio glanced at each other.

"Very well," Antonio mustered. "We were going to spend the night anyway."

Antonio and Baralt checked in. Half an hour later, they strode into a standard room. Father Arriaga sat down in a chair and waited. Meanwhile, Baralt slumped down on a bed while Antonio inspected everything. Baralt didn't allow the priest a chance to change his mind and said, "So, hermano, what papers are you going to share with us?"

Arriaga's face turned red. Hastily, he snapped open the briefcase. "First of all, don't call me *brother*! I'm doing this *only* to avoid a scandal!" He pulled out a manila file folder.

They stared at him in silence.

He held the file tightly in his hands. "I will deliver this letter to you *only* if you give me your word of honor to keep my name away from this ghastly letter!"

Baralt nodded. "Palabra de Dios."

Antonio followed. "Mi palabra sagrada."

He threw the file on the bed and sat back. "There!"

Baralt grabbed the file, opened it, and reviewed a photocopied page of a handwritten letter signed by Simón Bolívar and witnessed by Revérend.

> I, Simón Bolívar, Liberator of the Republic of Colombia, a native of the city of Caracas, in the Department of Venezuela, declare and order that, once deceased, my heart be transferred to the people of Cuzco, as proof

of my true affection, even in my last moments, for the heirs of the kingdom of the sun. December 10 1830.[1]

They stared at the letter in silence.

"Where's the original?" Antonio asked.

"I swear by the oath I've taken as a priest that it's a copy of what I found in the archive of the Cathedral!" Arriaga exclaimed. "It's a photocopy of another copy. I don't know where the original is."

Antonio paced.

Baralt glanced at the letter. "Many will say it's a fake like his letter to his cousin Fanny, Antonio, but that's not important." He rose and placed a hand on Antonio's shoulder. "What's important is that you have *something!*"

"I must find the original!"

The priest continued. "The copy in the Cathedral looks yellow enough to suggest that it was copied twenty years ago or more."

"Maybe when the original was moved to another site," Baralt suggested. He omitted the information conveyed by his contact in Santa Marta that the original was in a Vatican archive.

"Perhaps it was transferred to Rome," Father Arriaga offered. "I don't care what you do with it. I shouldn't have made a copy," he repeated.

"So why didn't you destroy it?" Antonio yelled, holding the copy and waving it in the air. "If it's so troublesome, why did you keep it?"

Baralt calmed him down. "There are no consequences, my friends."

Again, Antonio waved the letter in the priest's face. "Is this a ruse? Hmm? Are you trying to set me up?"

---

[1] Yo, Simón Bolívar, Libertador de la República de Colombia, natural de la ciudad de Caracas, en el Departamento de Venezuela, declaro y ordeno que, una vez muerto, mi corazón sea trasladado al pueblo de Cuzco, en prueba de mi verdadero afecto que, aún en mis últimos momentos, conservo a aquellos herederos del reino del sol. 10 de Diciembre de 1830.

"No," he answered calmly. "There are repercussions. I don't want publicity. I want to continue my work without being compromised by you or anyone else."

"So why are they looking for me?" Antonio yelled.

Father Arriaga stayed calm. "I don't know who's looking for you."

Antonio sat on the bed and glanced at Baralt, who understood Antonio's frustration. Perú's current indigenous population was 45 percent native Andean. They needed to hear this story. Spain's brutal exploitation of indigenous people was one obvious cataclysm, one that Rome probably wanted to hide; however, there was an equally important need to explore this story from the perspective of a Quechua like Antonio.

Antonio was correct in saying that the actors of yesterday were the actors of today; everything was connected beyond our space-time. The modern gold boom of Perú was a new version of the same forced labor of children and women of colonial times. In modern times, they were channeled into sex trafficking and collateral occupations. Males as young as seventeen were recruited or kidnapped from villages around Cuzco through threats, deceptive recruitment, or debt bondage.

"Nothing should be taken for granted," Baralt said. "Someone said, 'Cast off what doesn't serve you before it robs you of your life.' So take the letter to Cuzco. You can't take the heart, but you can take this letter."

CHAPTER 16

AMARU, COSMIC SERPENT

The following day began under water-choked clouds that refused to break. David walked into the kitchen and found Gloria making a fresh pot of coffee. Both could smell the approaching rain in the air. He took his place at the table without saying anything and waited for her to serve him a cup. She was aware that he had a lot on his mind.

"Have you eaten breakfast?" she asked as she placed the cup in front of him.

He nodded, taking a sip.

She looked awesome, and David acknowledged this fact as soon as she sat down in her customary place. She was dressed in an all-black linen dress with an open neck and flared sleeves that reached down to her elbows. The centerpiece of her outfit was a twenty-inch sterling silver and turquoise necklace, hand-strung with real beads that culminated in a three-inch pendant, all details forged by a Navajo artist of her hometown in New Mexico. She collected these necklaces, believing that turquoise brought her good luck, gave her energy, and kept her in good health. In addition, turquoise was a part of the soil of her homeland, mined from the time of the Aztecs, and, as a result, it gave her renewed energy, just like drinking water.

She smiled, accepting the compliment. After a few seconds, she asked, "So, you think Jonathan will have any problems?"

"No. Spoke to Karl. He approved Isabel's release without a bond. They're expecting Jonathan."

She got to the point. "Where is she going to stay?"

"With you."

She nodded. "Okay. So what plans do you have?"

"First, asylum."

"Think they'll give it to her?"

"No. We have to find Antonio."

"How?"

"I don't think it's going to be difficult."

She laughed. "Nothing is impossible for you, Mr. Levin!"

"Antonio and I have a mutual friend," he said. "He's not a real friend, but his family is a part of my network."

"Who?"

"Rafael Aguilar."

"The journalist?"

"Yes. In the meantime, we have to prepare Isabel for her interview. You can help her to focus on the right thing. She needs to make some sense. Frankly, her obsession with what happened to her family back in 1780 isn't going to help us."

She let out a chuckle. "We Navajo are often accused of clinging to the past, but it depends on who's telling the story. We live by values that are totally different from those of the mainstream. No disrespect intended toward you, Mr. Levin, but ours is another reality."

"I understand. She was kidnapped in Perú and held hostage in Spain. Things are beginning to make sense."

She shook her head. "Will that make any sense to the government?"

"You said that we have to face another reality. Genocide never makes sense, does it?" he said, somewhat somberly. "Hopefully, Dr. Peltier will guide us through some of Perú's historical bias against its Indians, something I know nothing about. Good grounding."

She was beginning to like the logic of his plan.

"We're going to record Dr. Peltier's comments, transcribe them into an affidavit, and give the affidavit to the government to support Isabel."

"And if they don't accept the affidavit?"

He grinned. "Just develop a record, Gloria. I don't care whether they reject it or not. We'll offer it."

*****

At the designated time, he took the awaited call from Dr. Barbara Peltier, informing her that Gloria was also on the line.

"Good to speak with both of you," Dr. Peltier answered in a high-pitched voice, not ideal for an expert witness, but she was ideal for David's objectives.

David quickly brought her up to date on Isabel's situation. She responded, "I also received your e-mail, Mr. Levin, and will begin with groundwork in order to explain a few of the fundamental ideological biases against people like Isabel Condorcanqui, whose bloodline has a lot of historical content."

"Go ahead, Dr. Peltier," he said.

"So, Isabel's ancestral grandfather, Juan Bautista, died in Buenos Aires in 1827. Has the government of Perú requested his remains?"

"No, from what I've gathered."

"What about any other descendants of those involved in the 1780 rebellion?"

"Fernando Condorcanqui, also referred to as Fernando Túpac Amaru."

"Relationship?"

"He was the youngest son of José Gabriel Condorcanqui."

"Túpac Amaru II?"

"Yes."

"He was Juan Bautista's nephew and Isabel's ancestral cousin, correct?"

"Yes."

"What happened to him?"

"He died in Madrid."

"When?"

"In 1798," Gloria interjected.

"Several centuries are a long time, enough time to ask for his remains," Dr. Peltier said. "Therefore, in view of the historical importance of the Condorcanqui family, it appears that the government of Perú has ignored Túpac Amaru II's immediate family."

David offered, "It appears that way even though Túpac Amaru II is regarded as an important figure in the country's history."

"Any other relatives of importance?"

"Fernando had two brothers," he answered, "one executed with his parents and the other who died on the way to Spain."

"Exiled?"

"Yes."

"There are no remains to claim?"

"I don't know, but Isabel believes that Fernando's tomb is in Madrid. In addition, her sister and parents died in a car accident about one year after the kidnapping," he added.

"How did she find out?" Dr. Peltier asked.

"Her handlers gave her the news."

"Does she know where they're buried?"

"No," Gloria answered.

David said, "It's a good point to investigate."

"It's interesting that we have a brother and a sister who are descendants of the founder of the Inca, Manco Cápac, each kidnapped by soldiers forty years ago. Where's the brother?"

"Maybe in Colombia," David answered.

"What's the story on the brother?"

"At first, they told her that he was killed while trying to escape from his captors. Recently her handlers told her that he was alive and that they would help her find him if she transferred to the United States."

"I'm sure that she was devastated when she was told that he'd been killed. More reason for her to resign herself to her captivity."

"This is also another reason she said, 'They killed Pachamama.'"

"Most likely," Dr. Peltier said. "Manco Cápac was brought into existence by the Sun God, Inti, and his sister, Quilla, according to the mythological data available. Quilla and Pachamama are integral parts of the Andean people's existence, Mother Moon and Mother Earth. These mythological facts can lead to an official bias against the Túpac Amaru family.

David asked, "How does myth support this bias? Isn't that a large leap in logic?"

"Mythology is real to these indigenous people. I would say that myth can bolster an ideology—for instance, an ideology viewed as antagonistic to the one held by those in power."

"The government has moved in the direction of recognizing Túpac Amaru II as a very important historical figure," he argued.

"Several years before the kidnappings," Dr. Peltier said, "the political environment changed. By the time Antonio and Isabel were kidnapped, several countries in South America began to turn against people like them."

"So, in your opinion, how does this ideological bias work against Isabel?"

"I can only give you the history, Mr. Levin. The most important part of this puzzle is that Antonio and Isabel are bloodline descendants of the mythical founder of the Inca, Manco Cápac. Every civilization has a mythical or real founder—for instance, Abraham."

"The Navajo have the Sun God and Changing Woman," Gloria said.

Dr. Peltier continued, "The Spanish Inquisition molded the Spanish state that governed colonial Perú, which led to the state of today."

"Yes, go on," David said.

"The Inquisition was at the center of the political development of the new Peruvian state. The program of the organized church and organized state was to displace Inti and Quilla, their descendants, and other potential separatist groups, like the Jews. Bolstered by the Inquisition, the state gave legitimacy to a new order that replaced Inti and Quilla. In Perú, the state inaugurated new approaches in order to centralize its power. *Autos de fé* were conducted for three centuries that led to public burnings and torture to get rid of potentially impure elements."

"But these *autos* weren't massive occurrences," David argued.

"These public events were part of a systematic campaign to inflict terror in the minds of Indians and secret Jews and any other subversives in order to force loyalty to the new state. Thus, we have the growth of an ideologically pure nation, free of any racial and religious opposition, perceived or real, defensive toward a separate Indian identity. The state became radicalized by applying a pro-European white bureaucracy, filtered down through the educational, political, and religious system that has survived until now."

"Our government will argue that those autos de fé are completely irrelevant because they're part of the past," he argued.

"We've modernized things in the United States because we prosecute people for crimes of hate, but they're still imbedded in our system—for instance, racially or gender-motivated murders. These hate crimes are seeded by past values. The repercussions remain real today."

He acknowledged her point.

She continued. "I'm going to try to explain how a culture keeps many old biases at an almost molecular level. We can call it an attack of our maturing human consciousness in spite of efforts to grow into something different. Past experiences mold that consciousness. First, there are the aggressors, and second, there are the victims. In the case of native Andeans, associative reactions of terror or shock are passed down through many generations because the Spanish restricted many fundamental things. It happened socially and economically, like ripping Indian fathers from their families and villages, killing them without a communal mourning process. José Gabriel Condorcanqui fought against taking the blood of their sacred mountains, the ancestral mother, for the export of silver to Spain without any deference to the land or to the people or to their values. Please keep in mind that all these things happened for centuries."

"And they continue with the slave trade."

"Yes. The biases imposed by the conquerors were beaten into the culture. The persecution of the indigenous separatist identity still exists. The slave trade of indigenous girls is one of many examples of this."

After a pause, Dr. Peltier continued. "Some would argue that Isabel's life is the result of what the Spanish system—ergo, today's system—is doing to these people. As you commented in your e-mail, Isabel is Pachamama, raped, plundered, demeaned, a reflection of the status of women who have been turned into outlaws for belonging to a class of people who can't get the protection of the state because the state is, psychologically speaking, still a Spanish colony and still very male oriented."

"Would you argue that it's intentional persecution?"

She responded, "Why did her kidnappers take her to Spain?"

"We don't know."

"How old was she?"

"About seventeen, eighteen," David answered.

"A child. They moved her to Spain when she was older to make it more difficult for her to get away. Conspiracies by the organized church and the organized state to stamp out dissent aren't things that have remained in the past. We've seen that with Franco in Spain and with the Dirty War in Argentina."

Gloria interrupted, "But why did they target Isabel in such a way?"

"The facts point to a machine that has outlived the democratic evolution of the world. Isabel poses a danger to the old establishment due to values that were set in precolonial times. According to the Spanish, the only ones who were witches were women, who were the key healers, birthers, and midwives in a world that lost its balance when the Spanish arrived. Andean society before that had a different perspective of how life worked. While the Spanish looked at life as good and evil with women as dangerous, a very simplistic version of the garden of Eden, the ancient Andean society treated women with greater respect, especially women of royal lineage and priestesses. Men, especially if they're members of a rational white supremacist culture, have a short fuse in understanding what happened in the Americas."

"Is it genetic?" Gloria asked.

"It's possible but mostly cultural. European-based families who don't share the heritage of indigenous people have a difficult time understanding those values. Village female healers," she added, "were persecuted in Europe, and the battle spilled into the Americas, hence the way and manner that modern political, religious, and even health institutions view indigenous women because they had a lot of power in the community. Isabel is a symbol of what the Spanish feared the most in the Americas, an indigenous woman with a very powerful lineage, associated with the mythological foundation of the region."

"I don't think we can argue that Isabel is being persecuted as a witch," David mentioned.

"I'm not suggesting that," Dr. Peltier answered, "but please understand that the European witch craze of the sixteenth century—the forced confessions, tortures, public burnings, the campaign against any underground opposition—was an expression of European political thought, which was transferred to Andean society. Women were the most susceptible to stereotypes. This mentality became encoded in the state's agenda of cementing its power. The colonizers created institutions that tied Peruvians to Spain, and the first institution was religion. The first targets were women because of their importance in communal life. They were royal and served as priestesses."

"I can't make this a case of religious persecution, either," he argued.

"Maybe it's too farfetched," Dr. Peltier conceded, "but you have to understand Pachamama."

"Maybe so," he replied.

Gloria stepped in. "I can understand it because of the way Christians persecuted my people."

"Yes, Christian Indian Residential Schools were a part of the reprogramming."

David said, "Please continue, Dr. Peltier."

"The Spanish couldn't accept the Indians' great respect for the sun, moon, trees, ocean, rivers, etcetera, because they found a tradition of demonology in every *huaca* in Andean society ..."

"What is a huaca?" he asked.

"A shrine. Some of them are very simple. The Spanish thought women were interacting with demons through these shrines to nature, Mother Earth, Pachamama. Juana Icha was tried for making a pact with the devil. One of the witnesses against her said that she worshipped the earth and the stars and cried to the waters."

She added, "The Inca saw a dualistic universe in which men and women reciprocated each other and both complemented nature, including the supernatural. Ayni, balance and reciprocity, was central to the existence of the individual and the collective, therefore to the individual and the group, both with nature, nature with them, the living and the dead, and vice versa. A requirement for ayni was offerings—in other words, feeding the spiritual forces."

"Isabel mentioned ayni," Gloria offered.

"Yes. Colonial Inca ground corn and seashells and blew the substance onto sacred shrines, and they also blew coca leaves to the sun and placed corn beer on the graves of their ancestors. Imbalances made *amaru*, the cosmic serpent, shake the earth. This was the physical-cosmic reality of the Andean people."

"My goodness, that sounds familiar," Gloria interjected. "Are you speaking of the serpent of the Aztecs too?"

"These are mythical themes that run through the great civilizations of the Americas, the Aztec, Inca, and Maya. All of them were conquered and colonized by the Spanish. The Spanish took advantage of prophesy. We have to understand the perspectives of each group, the conqueror and the conquered, in order to make some sense of why some groups are persecuted today."

CHAPTER 17

THE VILLAGE

"It was easy for the Inquisition to associate the cosmic serpent of the Inca with Satan given the story in Genesis," David said to Gloria as soon as they hung up.

He added, "This threat was expanded with the name of Túpac Amaru, who led that powerful revolt, further distorting the meaning to include subversion. That's why Antonio and Isabel Condorcanqui are associated with this interpretation—because their family's name is also Túpac Amaru."

Gloria nodded. "Their bloodline is associated with the cosmic serpent."

"The serpent is still venerated by the Andean indigenous people and feared by modern institutions."

"People do perverse things in order to protect their icons," Gloria noted, thinking of her own Navajo symbols.

"The Andean indigenous community has extremely powerful values that, understandably, can be threatening, so a permanent state of ideological submission is used to keep everyone in check," David said. It was exactly what the local weed enforcement authorities were doing to the Mexicans on North Bishop Avenue, but he decided not to complicate matters by mentioning that. He needed to keep everything as simple as possible. Instead, he added, "I'm just having a hard time understanding the cosmology in this discussion."

"These are things that are difficult to explain to a Western, rational mind."

"Unless you're a Navajo Indian," he ventured with a grin.

"A mountain can be just as sacred as a man-made cathedral. Forces of nature are members of the assembly, not just humans. Collectives include a corresponding life system."

He remained silent.

"In other words, the village in which we live is larger than a physical village. The Andean people don't believe in Pachamama because they *are* Pachamama. You said that yourself, Mr. Levin."

"Isabel is a symbol of Pachamama, that's all."

"It isn't such a mystery. Take it to another level. There's no concept of faith or belief in what already exists. There's no punishment for disbelieving, simply a manifestation of something that is out of alignment. A few minutes ago, Dr. Peltier spoke about huacas. Huacas are the dwelling place of the gods, Pachamama among them."

"I see that you've been doing some research."

She nodded. "Humans expand the physical so that the divine can be manifested through their prayers. Ritual is part of everyday indigenous life. The regular acknowledgement of the divine, in our terms, is to strengthen the alliance with the supernatural world that we take for granted. We live in a universal village. You do that in your Hebrew prayers. We have the power to transform the universe because we *are* the universe. I don't believe it's that strange."

He took that in. He reflected, "The cosmic serpent of the Andeans is a different conversation from the serpent in Genesis, but it was the only filter that the Spanish had, even though the village is the planet."

"Excuse me?

"Joseph Campbell."

"The Spanish didn't understand the *cosmic* side of the serpent as the Inca did, Mr. Levin. The filters are expanding, but these ideological biases still exist, which is why Isabel still poses a threat to the current establishment."

CHAPTER 18

RED MOON RISING

As soon as their conference ended, Gloria left David's office and returned to her own, where she found Jonathan and Isabel waiting for her. Crossing her threshold, she extended a hand to Isabel, who wore a dark blue cotton smock.

"How are you?" Gloria asked in Spanish.

Isabel nodded.

Jonathan handed over a manila file and said, "They said that we should make an appointment for her credible fear interview because her permit may be terminated in thirty days."

"What?"

"If her captors reach a plea with the government, they may be out of here in thirty days. That's what the ICE officer said."

Gloria guessed that they were putting pressure on David.

Meanwhile, Isabel focused her attention on the statue of the Virgin of Guadalupe behind Gloria, then at the Diné Pride sign above the statue.

Gloria returned to her chair. "That means that we have to prepare you, Isabel."

"¿Cómo?" she asked, although Gloria and Jonathan had said everything in Spanish.

"We have to go back and speak to them about your kidnapping."

She frowned. "Haven't we spoken enough? What do they want from me?"

"The procedure in this country involves an interview in order to determine if you have a well-founded fear of persecution by returning to Perú based on all the bad things that have happened to you and to your family. The same applies to Spain. Remember, I asked you if you were willing to return to Perú or to Spain, and you said no."

She stared at the statue. "That's Pachamama."

Gloria agreed. "She's the Virgin of Guadalupe, but she's also known as Tonantzin. To us, the Navajo, she's ShimáNahasdzáán."

"We offer seashells and coca leaves to Pachamama."

"We offer her things too," she replied while glancing at Jonathan.

"What do those words mean?" Isabel asked, pointing at the wall.

"Diné is the name of my people," she answered, "and 'Diné Pride' means that we're proud to be Diné."

"I'm Quechua. I'm Condorcanqui. Sometimes I ride on the rays of the moon in order to go to heaven where my ancestors live. I'm also Túpac Amaru."

Gloria and Jonathan stared at each other. Gloria said, "I know, Isabel. We discussed it with a person who knows a lot about Perú. Right, Jonathan?"

He grinned, responding, "Yes," without expanding the conversation. He was thirty-five years old and had been with the firm for ten years. He was a younger, more conservative version of David Levin.

Isabel continued her inspection. "I like your necklace."

Gloria took it off and placed it around her neck. "This is yours."

She gave her a startled look and placed a hand over the pendant. "We make silver jewelry too."

Gloria returned to her chair and grinned. "We have many things in common."

"This necklace has emotions," she added, stroking the turquoise beads.

"It was made by a friend of mine."

"Silver is the blood of Pachamama."

"You just said that you ride the rays of the moon. We believe that too. Women carry the moon inside their wombs. We're the powerful caretakers of the village. We know how to work with herbs and plants. We know chants that bring medicine to our people. I'd like to invite you to stay at my house so that we can learn from each other."

She nodded. "It's a wonderful idea."

"And then, you can come here, and we can work on what you're going to tell the government officer. What do you think?"

Isabel grinned. "I know what you're trying to do."

Not one to chase after innuendos, Gloria asked, "What am I trying to do?"

She shrugged. "To train me."

"Exactly. We don't want you to leave if you're afraid to. I know that Pachamama is claiming her children, Isabel. The clan mothers want their children to return home. You and I have to practice so that the officer will understand your story because, frankly, they don't understand Indians, much less Indian women like you and me, and much less women like you."

"My ancestor, the sun, changed into human form in order to live with humankind. His sister was Quilla, the moon, and she's the mother of our first king, Manco Cápac. I'm their blood descendant. No one understands that."

"That's what I'm trying to say. Not many understand that relationship. We Indians say that the red moon is rising."

She nodded. "I'm Quilla, the white moon."

"Yes, the moon has many phases, but many don't believe it."

"Then, what's the point of talking to those people?"

"You have to speak like them."

"Will the officer speak Spanish?"

Both Gloria and Jonathan nodded.

"So what's the problem?"

"The problem," Gloria replied, "is that their way of life isn't our way of life. The world right now fails to see that we have ancestral responsibilities. When a Navajo is born, the child belongs to the clan of the mother. I was raised to trust my womb even though those in power taught that our moon time wasn't sacred, that we women were empty vessels not capable of wisdom. The official church replaced Mother Earth. Women were taught to keep their daughters submissive. So our clans grew older while enduring centuries of pain, a pain that came from a place where humans hold their wisdom, and that place grew more and more empty."

She nodded.

"It's the pain of the mothers, which is the pain of our people," Gloria added.

"No one has gone through more pain than I have," Isabel responded.

"My ancestors were taken on a Long Walk to a place called Fort Sumner, away from the love and protection of our holy people in the mountains. We became very sick and we starved. The sacred rainbow no longer protected us."

"Where do your holy people live?" Isabel asked.

"According to my elders, when we were created, four mountains and four rivers were designated as our home, but we were taken away from there because of the war with the white man."

"My holy people are in Cuzco. That's why my brother and I were taken. We're descendants of the holy people."

Gloria nodded. "My ancestors were eventually allowed to return to our homeland, exhausted and feeling great pain. As I said, we almost lost our wisdom, but it survived because our white-haired people didn't forget it. It remained hidden through many layers of existence." She smiled.

Isabel returned the smile.

"You and I must be very smart about how we maneuver things and how we say things to the official. The red moon *is* rising because we're smarter now. You have the blood of the holy people. We have more resources. The red moon will pave the way for the white moon."

"How can I protect myself? What do I have?"

"You have what you have, Isabel. You have me and Jonathan and Mr. Levin. We're your family. Together, we'll find a way to tell your story because there's a realignment that's taking place. The

Western world is beginning to understand our story. We have to practice so that they can see that we all have an inner dialogue with Pachamama."

Seconds later, David walked in and introduced himself to Isabel. He added, "I think I'll find your brother ..."

She suppressed her emotions as she stroked the necklace in silence.

He continued. "There's a man in Mexico who knows Antonio. I spoke with his family in Venta Prieta. His family is expecting him tomorrow."

"Are you sure he knows where Antonio is?" Gloria asked.

He nodded. "The timing couldn't be better. Rafael Aguilar is a key to unlocking this forty-year puzzle."

CHAPTER 19

RAFAEL AGUILAR

Visiting his family consumed several days until the goal of driving to Tierra Blanca placed Rafael outside of his ordinary affairs. The drive north triggered a lot to think about—the call from David Levin, for instance. David had been succinct: "I'm representing a relative of Antonio Condorcanqui here in Dallas."

"Who?" Rafael asked, also wondering how David got his family's telephone number.

"Isabel Condorcanqui," David replied. "I think you and I need to have a personal meeting."

"Where?"

"Where are you going to be in three days?"

Rafael glanced at his wristwatch. "I'm leaving for Tierra Blanca tomorrow."

"Where's Tierra Blanca?"

"Northeastern Guanajuato. How about meeting me at noon on Friday in the city of Guanajuato in front of Teatro Juarez?"

"How can we stay in touch?"

"I have a temporary phone." Rafael dictated the number.

By high morning on the following day, Rafael was driving into the landscape of the Cerro people, as his Otomí brothers and sisters of Tierra Blanca were known. Before he approached the town, a herd of goats burst in front of his father's pickup truck and raced across the open road into a roadside ravine, followed by a couple of Otomí lads. He stared at them and at the arid hills, whose history hovered over like an old shadow, because everything happened very slowly. He was swept by an experience that he called inspiration.

At that moment, he absorbed the latent energy in everything, even the asphalt road, a nonlocal mind-set that took him beyond everything he felt, saw, or thought. The breath of the hills seeped into his skin, while intuitive data that traveled beyond the ages went to his quiet self. Maybe it was the same path that folk heroes walked when they reached the summit of their dreams or when they clambered up narrow trails that led them to other trails.

For now, though, he relaxed and allowed himself to be bewitched by the captivating spell of the magical hills whose colors mixed together under a blue sky. He was about to walk on the flesh and bones of the earth, carried by her breath and washed by her waters. It was a place where the Otomí came back to when they grew apart from their souls and where their profound emotional and physical scars were transformed into great lessons.

The Otomí people of the hills around Santo Tomás de Tierra Blanca, founded in 1536 by an Otomí chieftain, were still showing their relentless drive to survive while maintaining their customs and their mixed Catholic-indigenous belief system. Nineteen Indian communities with a history of kidnapping those politicians who really offended them were subsisting on farming and goat herding, though they also ventured into new markets, creating opportunities for camping, hiking, trekking, and even spiritual *limpias* for tourists, along with arts, crafts, and their traditional herbs and textiles.

The eclectic main plaza of Tierra Blanca was dedicated to Miguel Hidalgo. Looking back at their history, the Otomí were famous for their adaptive skills. Although the Otomí could be fierce fighters, they helped the empire of the Spanish as middlemen who brokered agreements with warring tribes. With the new economic landscape that arrived with the discovery of gold near Mexico City soon after 1521, along with the great silver lodes of Guanajuato, San Luis Potosí, and Zacatecas, they moved northward. Querétaro was founded by an Otomí chieftain, baptized with the name of Hernando de la Tapia. His son contributed to the discovery of the famous silver mines of San Luis Potosí, named after Potosí Mountain in the Andes. Rafael and Antonio had immediately connected over shared memories of two silver mines in very distant lands.

Spurred by these thoughts, Rafael decided to drive to the city of Dolores Hidalgo after a late lunch with local Otomí officials. He wanted to wrap his mind around the history of this old mining center that was part of the old Spanish silver road and the pulpit of Miguel Hidalgo y Costilla's "The Cry of Dolores." Hidalgo's cry had ignited the movement of independence against Spain almost exactly thirty years after José Gabriel began his rebellion in Tinta, Perú.

The drive to the epicenter of Mexico's first major insurrection brought thoughts of Antonio Condorcanqui, like a ghost bolted to the passenger seat of the pickup truck. Antonio often said, "One doesn't have to be an Indian to listen to the heart of Pachamama." His indigenous people believed that everything affected everyone and everything at all times in the same way that children affected their parents and the parents affected their children, while the living affected the dead. Everyone continued to coexist in this cosmic onion.

While Rafael drove to the city of Guanajuato through a sierra named after Perú's capital, Santa Rosa de Lima, he took note of another shared memory—the presence of thousands of Peruvian miners who traveled the Pan-American silver route and settled in these mountains. They brought their skills and families and botanical knowledge, such as the Peruvian pepper tree, otherwise called pirul, which was a cornerstone of the traditional medicinal practices used by the indigenous people of Mexico today. The pirul was also associated with Mother Moon as far north as Arizona, California, and New Mexico. In Rafael's mind, the law of ayni, as Antonio would say, brought the Quechua, Aymara, Otomí, Nahuatl, Chichimeca, Yaqui, Apache, and hundreds of other native groups together through nature.

Mexico's independence movement was a part of the same onion occupied by José Gabriel Condorcanqui and, later, Simón Bolívar, who stated in 1815 that the Mexicans were resolved to avenge their ancestors or to follow them to the grave. Some called the onion natural law, while others described it as the heart of the dancing woman with a thin waist whose head was in North America and whose womb was nestled in the Amazon and in the Andes.

A mantra of the Spanish conquerors was that their god had replaced all the others, when, in reality, no god replaced another because it was all one to the indigenous people of the Americas. José Gabriel Condorcanqui, Simón Bolívar, and Miguel Hidalgo lived in different physical worlds, yet as members of the same soul family, tried to make some sense of events that followed a common subconscious stream.

In fact, Miguel Hidalgo wasn't an Indian but a creole, or criollo, a person born in America of Spanish descent, conversant in local native languages and, like José Gabriel, a product of Jesuit schooling.

Hidalgo passionately objected to the way Spain restricted local economic growth among the Indians. Once he settled himself as the parish priest of Dolores in 1802, he began a campaign to teach them about making bricks and pottery and leather goods, teaching them to use the natural resources of the environment to grow their own food. He set out to encourage them to create their own natural ecohabitat.

Hidalgo was an ordained priest with a nativist agenda who objected to the privileges bestowed upon the Spanish-born residents of the New World, the *gachupines*, and so he took the banner of the Virgin of Guadalupe, known as the brown Virgin or Tonantzin of Atotonilco.

In Perú, José Gabriel Condorcanqui used the *mascaipacha*, the Incan tasseled wool crown with feathers of the Corequenque bird, the greatest symbol of power of his royal ancestors. Both he and Hidalgo led massive popular movements. Both were beheaded by the Spanish after a brutal execution—Hidalgo by a firing squad, and José Gabriel by dismemberment, though ineffective. His torso was burnt. His head was placed on a pike at the main entrance of Cuzco and then sent to Tinta, while one of his arms was shipped to Tungasuca, the other to Carabaya, and his legs to Livitica and Santa Rosa, for public viewing.

Thirty years afterward, the Spanish followed the same systematic campaign to enforce loyalty by terror and sent Hidalgo's head to the city of Guanajuato's granary, the Alhóndiga de Granaditas. Along with three others that belonged to fellow insurgents, his head was hung inside of an iron cage from one of the outside corners of the granary. No one removed his head for nine years and ten months, until the war was won by the Mexicans.

It was apparent that both Hidalgo and José Gabriel had a deep grasp of their own regions. Both understood that the miners of Mexico and Perú endured the same brutality, such as deep and unsafe narrow tunnels and shafts, flimsy tools, undependable wooden ladders, underground floods, asphyxiation, and the total absence of medical treatment. They also objected to the massive exploitation of natives by the forced draft and forced purchase and production of European products. "Me costó un Perú," or "It cost me a Perú," was part of the world's explanation for the unprecedented cost that Perú paid for its gold and silver. Eight million Indians had died in Potosí Mountain alone during the colonial era. The Quechua people called it "the mountain that eats men."

Quechua and Aymara Indians were exported to Mexico, where the highly stressed Mexican workers were subjected to the same acute hunger, accidents, lung disease, and exposure to lethal smallpox and measles, as well as to *cocolitzli*, a native Mexican virus. These and many more problems wiped out entire native communities in central Mexico. By some accounts, the native population of this region was reduced from twenty-two million to two million native Mexicans in fewer than eighty years after the arrival of the Spanish.

It was an intercontinental tragedy that spawned the war of independence that, to this day, was erroneously defined by many modern-day scholars as isolated regional incidents. They said that the Incan rebellion of José Gabriel Condorcanqui, for example, had no relationship with the movements led by Miguel Hidalgo and Simón Bolívar three decades later.

It seemed surreal that these arguments were ignoring the invisible yet deep relationship between the creoles and Indians of various regions of the Americas. But then, colonial Spain's divide-and-conquer measures built inner operating systems that, although ineffective in stopping the struggle for independence, continued to survive to this day. These systems were never meaningfully redefined after the war and conveniently pushed the spirit memory into some kind of abyss that even Simón Bolívar challenged by recognizing the close relationship between the native collective soul. He said, "[Hidalgo's] use of the Virgin of Guadalupe as the queen of the patriots aptly produced a passionate fervor for the sacred cause of freedom." According to Bolívar, it was a strategy that only the cleverest prophet could inspire. He understood the soul memory of the Mexicans.

*****

Twenty hours later, Rafael arrived at his hotel on the edge of Jardín de la Unión. It was his third visit to the city of Guanajuato, a place with hillside tapestry of multicolored colonial architecture, congested alleyways, narrow streets, stairs, great cathedrals and churches, balconies, and fountains that reminded him of Rome and, in many conspicuous and inconspicuous ways, of Cartagena.

The city's subterranean history always spurred Rafael's creative restlessness. Once he was settled in his hotel room, he strode along the city's sidewalks, savoring its famous vegetable soups, fresh vegetable juices, mole, *nopales*, artistic graffiti, people bearing bread and tortillas on their heads, intense crowds distracted by their own casual conversations, painters offering impromptu portraits, folk and mariachi musicians and children playing accordions, and a noisy ambience fed by *estudiantinas*, student minstrels who sang Spanish medieval songs.

He met David Levin at the designated time on the following day. Teatro Juarez was a few paces from Rafael's hotel. For a September day, it was cool. It was also early for lunch, but he had planned it this way. He led David to the restaurant, where they sat at a table on a balcony facing the Church of San Diego and ordered two beers and taquitos.

Once the beer bottles were served, each swiped a piece of lime around the mouth of the bottle and took a gulp. David waved toward Teatro Juarez. "Strange to find the nine Muses here," he said casually, amusing himself with the sculptures of the Greeks' goddesses of music, song, and dance, lauded by Homer. He reached into the pocket of his tan leather jacket and pulled out his passport and business card.

Rafael examined them briefly and smiled. "I checked out your website. You've been a lawyer for a long time."

David grinned. "Maybe too long."

"Where are you staying?"

"Here."

"I'm staying here too."

David laughed.

Rafael didn't offer information about his belief in indirect revelation. It was better to leave it this way. "I made a reservation for lunch in another restaurant. It's across the plaza."

"The one with the piano?"

"Yes, you're familiar with it?" Rafael asked while taking a sip of his beer. "The head waiter will provide us with a good table."

David nodded. "Had dinner there last night. Piano music inside, mariachi music outside," he said, returning his passport to his pocket.

Rafael pointed at the Church of San Diego and added, "Most of the early churches had an atrium in the front, used for the evangelization of Indians. Sometimes it was forced by tying them to trees and piercing their breasts or pectorals. When the atrium finished its purpose, it was used as a cemetery for the poor until the government started to convert each one into a public park."

"So the Jardín de la Unión was used as a cemetery?"

Rafael nodded. "I just came from Dolores Hidalgo. The front of Miguel Hidalgo's church shares the same history."

David examined Rafael's wide forehead, strong brown eyes, square jaw, and relaxed appearance, and he liked what he saw. His first impressions were usually on the mark. He saw someone who was driven, who was practical yet idealistic, who fraternized easily with people yet was also serious. He was tall for a man who was one-half Otomí, but then his height wasn't extremely uncommon. "So where do I start?" he asked.

Casting a glance around the restaurant, Rafael offered, "I have no idea." He leaned over the edge of the table, his eyes searching for the right interaction that would produce the effect he expected. He managed a careful nod. "Try telling me something about Isabel Condorcanqui."

"Isabel Condorcanqui Pacha," he began, "born in Tungasuca fifty-seven years ago, was kidnapped at the age of seventeen years by soldiers, or men who appeared to be soldiers, near her private girls' school in Cuzco, put in a prison cell by herself for a couple of days, during which time she was raped and probably sodomized, then shipped to Pomacanchi where she was carried into a truck with women and children. The truck drove them to Lima."

Rafael swallowed hard. He raised the bottle and drank from it until he emptied it. He ordered another one.

David continued describing Isabel's ordeal from Lima to Ceuta without interruption except for when the taquitos were served. "And then," he concluded, "the patriarch of the household in which she lived died. Soon after that, her handlers told her that they would help her to find her brother if she agreed to go to the United States." He paused, scrutinizing Rafael, who was already into his third beer. No reaction was expected from someone who was justifiably guarded.

David caught his breath. "Am I going too fast?"

He shook his head. "No. Life is stranger than fiction."

"I don't have much in terms of hard facts, but she's been examined by a psychiatrist, and under hypnosis she gave the same details, including the name of her brother."

"So," Rafael asked, "how did my name come up?"

"I tapped into your articles through the magazine *Revista Once.*" He omitted Karl Segal's involvement.

"Ah. And how did you make the connection with Antonio Condorcanqui?"

"I didn't. It was guesswork. I know it was a stretch, but you call him Antonio, El Condor. When Isabel identified her brother, I made the connection," he said.

"How did you get my family's telephone number?"

"Through my temple in Dallas."

"How did you know I'm Jewish?"

David grinned. "Jewish genealogy is my field of interest."

He pressed on. "Aguilar? It's a very Spanish name."

"Venta Prieta is part of your ancestral fingerprint, not to mention the information you gave in the articles about the Inquisition."

He shrugged. "Everyone writes about the Inquisition."

"It's the tone of your articles. In any event, you mentioned the persecution against Jews more than once."

"That's not unusual," he answered with a smile.

"How about a dozen times?"

It was a debatable point. Rafael decided to return to the conversation. "What else?"

David reached into his shirt pocket and extracted a white envelope. He pulled out two passport photos, placed them across on the table, and waited.

Rafael grabbed them and began to carefully scan them. After a couple of minutes, he raised the photo in his right hand. "This one is Antonio's sister. Same face except for her nose because his is more prominent and hooked. Antonio wears his hair long, usually in a ponytail, and it's graying, but he doesn't look his fifty-four years."

David nodded. "She's been through hell and back."

"Antonio says that she never tried to contact him."

"Her captors told her that he was killed while trying to escape his kidnappers."

"Good way to control her," Rafael replied.

David didn't rush in with a comment.

"Who's the other woman?" Rafael asked, waving the photo in his left hand. "She looks like Isabel. They could pass for sisters except for the color of their eyes."

"Actually, she's Gloria Dolii García. I brought the photo because she may travel to Colombia to interview Antonio—of course, if this is necessary."

"Antonio may not agree to it."

"True, but it's always better to be prepared."

"So you're showing me her photo in that event."

David nodded. "She's an attorney who's helping me with Isabel's case." He munched on a nacho and added, "She's half Navajo."

"She's a very good-looking woman," Rafael offered.

"Widowed with three grown children."

"Ah."

"She's preparing Isabel for the asylum interview." He went on to describe Isabel's arrest and her current status as a witness against her captors, omitting everything related to her stay in a psychiatric ward, not because he intended to keep it a secret but because he wanted to spare Rafael the drama.

Hoping that his instincts were correct, David continued describing her highly charged allegations that officials associated with the government of Perú were after her and her family. "She says that her ancestral grandfather was Juan Bautista Condorcanqui, who was arrested in 1783 and sent to Ceuta until he returned to Buenos Aires in 1822, and that he tried to return to Cuzco but wasn't allowed by Simón Bolívar."

"I know the story."

"She insists that there's a systematic campaign of isolation of the Condorcanqui family, and that's why she was sent to Ceuta." He kept his eyes on Rafael, who didn't flinch. "Is this true?"

He didn't answer the question directly but said, "Juan Bautista died the seventh of September of 1827 in Buenos Aires. Almost everyone in Perú accepts the fact that his father, Miguel Condorcanqui, was also the father of José Gabriel Condorcanqui. They had different mothers. That's well documented. Even the fact that the priest of

Pomacanchi, described as Pomacachi by Juan Bautista, set fire to his house and poured salt over its ashes. Juan Bautista dictated his memoirs, which were published before he died."

"Interesting. I searched for his book, but it's difficult to get."

Rafael shrugged. "It's only available through some universities or the national archives of Argentina."

"Is it available in Perú?"

"I don't know." After eating another taquito, he added, "A few have challenged Juan Bautista's identity, but he received a government pension in Buenos Aires as the half-brother of José Gabriel Túpac Amaru. So far, many scholars are on his side."

David remained silent.

Rafael took out his phone and tapped into his e-mail, opening a folder that contained more information about Juan Bautista. He showed the content to David, who tried to read it but raised his head. "It's in Spanish."

"Sorry," Rafael said, taking the phone and pulling up another file. He handed the phone over again, adding, "This is an English version of the letter written on May fifteenth of 1825 to Bolívar, from a book titled *The Túpac Amaru and Catarista Rebellion*. The book offers an anthology of original sources collected by some American scholars who translated them into English."

David reviewed the content. The letter ended with, "I, sir, considering the pleasurable hope of breathing the air of my homeland ... [T]he incalculable grief and hardships [I have suffered] would seem as nothing if, before my eyes close, I might see my Liberator, and with this comfort I could go to my grave ... Juan Bautista Túpac Amaru.

He glanced up. "It doesn't sound like a plea Bolívar would have ignored, especially from an old man."

"Exactly."

"So, how do I make the link between Juan Bautista and his Incan lineage?"

"There's no strong connection except what survives of José Gabriel's litigation over his ancestral rights and an order by a Judge

Areche in Cuzco dated sometime after the execution of José Gabriel. The order implicates Juan Bautista as his half-brother and as an accomplice. Of course, when he was first arrested in 1781, Juan Bautista denied the relationship, but he was exiled two years later anyway. When he came back from Ceuta, he reclaimed his Túpac Amaru ancestry, stating that he was the fifth grandchild of Huayna Cápac. I don't know how you would describe it in your culture."

"Great-great-great-great-grandson," David answered.

"A few Peruvian scholars will connect Isabel and Antonio with Juan Bautista. In addition, she was sent to Ceuta, as if someone was trying to make a point, don't you think?"

"Yes."

Rafael remained silent until he waved at a waiter. "Let's continue this conversation while we lunch."

CHAPTER 20

THE BIRTH OF A REVOLUTIONARY

The other restaurant's table was more amenable to their conversation. It was inside the building at a discreet distance from the noisy pedestrian walk adjacent to the Jardín de la Unión. Most of the patrons looked like tourists. As soon as the men sat down, each ordered an espresso to subdue the effects of the beer. Rafael also ordered some *bocados* and red wine. It was obvious that he enjoyed this ritual.

He grinned. "Good atmosphere, don't you think?"

David remained silent.

"I have a room at the hotel," Rafael said, "that has access to a private terrace. We can go there after lunch. If that doesn't work, we can find another place."

"This city isn't very quiet."

"Yes. Have you been here before?"

"Many of my clients are from Guanajuato."

"Do you drive or come by air?"

"It varies. I used a private jet this time."

After a brief pause, Rafael continued their tête-à-tête. "Antonio wasn't born a revolutionary," he explained. "He was kidnapped while he was walking home from his school. Several men jumped out of a Jeep Cherokee and tried to force him into it. He was strong for his age and was able to run away. They were dressed in green fatigues, but, to this day, he doesn't know if they were Peruvian soldiers or not."

"Maybe they were Peruvians," David offered.

"Perú's government was headed by General Velasco Alvarado, who was a populist and very pro-Túpac Amaru," Rafael added. "Velasco's government was the first one to make Quechua an official language. He even issued notes with José Gabriel's image. Maybe that's the reason he was deposed."

"When?"

"It was in 1975."

"So, who do you think sent the soldiers?"

"There's a lot of evidence that points to Chile."

"What's the evidence?"

"It's common knowledge," Rafael answered.

"When did the kidnapping happen?"

"On October 2, 1973, almost a month after the coup against President Salvador Allende."

"I recall that coup," David said.

"General Augusto Pinochet led it. It took place on September 11, 1973."

"So why would General Pinochet be interested in Antonio and Isabel?"

Rafael frowned. "Call it an ideological cleansing. We've had a lot of those. The Cold War was peaking in South America. Uruguay had exploded into a civil war with the Tupamaros rallying behind the peasants and trade unions. The movement took its name from José Gabriel Condorcanqui, or Túpac Amaru II, so, in a way, it implicated Antonio's family in spite of their neutrality. In addition, as I said, Velasco Alvarado was a populist who recognized the power of the indigenous base, and he was aligning his government with Cuba and the Soviets. Pinochet started his movement before Velasco was ousted."

David nodded. "Guilt by association, I see."

"Yes, we have a habit of going to the far right or to the far left. We have a problem with staying somewhere in the center. So, Pinochet began his own extreme right-wing revolution with the coup against Allende; in fact, he started the execution and burial of people in mass graves and improvised concentration camps as soon as he took control of Chile. His motivation was to lead a movement against Communism, hence also against potential enemies of the state. I think Antonio and Isabel were swept away by Pinochet's paranoia. It was a natural reaction. His secret geoalliance brought six countries together with North American support, and he called it Operation Condor."

"I can understand why Antonio has sourced those articles," David said. "So, returning to the reason for the kidnapping, the Condorcanqui family posed a threat to Pinochet's movement."

"Naturally, Pinochet and his allies perceived them as a threat. In addition, the Andean condor is the national bird of Chile. Maybe Pinochet felt that Perú was a threat to his domination of the region. He removed Isabel and Antonio and their family and then removed General Velasco."

"The eagle is the symbol of Mexico and the United States."

"Yes."

"Symbols speak louder than words," David offered.

"True," Rafael replied.

"Looks like their parents' car accident in 1974 was no accident."

"By their lineage, Antonio and Isabel represent the mythological founders of the Inca—the Sun God, Inti, and his sister, Quilla, or Mother Moon, who parented Manco Cápac, the first Inca."

The server placed their lunch on the table.

"Where was Antonio when his family perished?"

"Antonio was fighting his underground war in Uruguay, but the Tupamaros were in the process of taking their guerrilla movement into other countries, such as Argentina." Rafael paused to consume a few rolls of beef. "Pinochet's secret alliance," he added, "was made official in late 1975 with the name of the First Inter-American Meeting of National Intelligence. It took place in Santiago, Chile."

"Was Perú a member?"

"No, but Perú was never isolated from Pinochet's tentacles. The other members of the alliance were Argentina, Brazil, Bolivia, Uruguay, and Paraguay. As its name implies, intelligence sharing was the main goal, even though it brought more than that because all interested parties participated in joint tracking, capture, imprisonment, torture, extradition, and, ultimately, execution of dangerous political subversives, even nonviolent ones, without following either national or international laws."

"How would Isabel's kidnappers get a certified copy of her birth certificate?" David asked.

He frowned. "There was a lot of intelligence sharing, although it's probable that someone in the government cooperated with Pinochet's people, or was bribed."

"Isabel spent a year in Brazil as a domestic slave," David said.

"Not strange considering that Brazil was a member of Pinochet's alliance." Rafael paused. "When did she arrive in Spain?"

"In 1974."

"Franco died a year later."

David remained silent.

Rafael continued. "This joint security operation drew all of its members into political assassinations of suspected subversives to an unprecedented scale, and I say *unprecedented* with a caveat because we have a history of genocide in this continent that goes back to European rule. There are many parallels with the past, including the kidnapping of children of impure persons who were disappeared, murdered, or jailed, to mention a few."

"Was Isabel sent to Spain for that reason?"

"It shows a pattern of persecution. She wasn't a child, per se, when she reached Spain, correct? However, she was abducted at the age of seventeen. Nonetheless, Spain was an appropriate destination for her, especially Ceuta, because the infrastructure was still contaminated with Franco's agenda. It was isolated."

"It's difficult to understand how she was held as a domestic slave for so many years," David said.

Rafael shook his head. "Not really. About three hundred thousand children of ideologically unacceptable persons, considered Reds, were unlawfully sequestered by the Franco regime and placed in what they considered suitable homes. They say that the Spanish Roman Catholic church played a key role in Franco's social services structure—for instance, hospitals, schools, and orphanages. Amnesty laws, generally known as the Pacto de Olvido, forgetting Franco's crimes, have made it almost impossible to investigate the culprits even though the Ministry of Justice is taking them on a case-by-case basis. In any event, Antonio and I have tried to hint at the existence of this same agenda in Argentina—"

David interrupted, "I read that article."

"—because the same thing happened and Antonio lived through it. Conservative religious cells encouraged the clandestine trafficking of children of subversives in Argentina. This type of cleansing goes back to the Inquisition. This is nothing new. Pinochet and his allies didn't want another José Gabriel Condorcanqui and Micaela Bastidas."

"Who's Micaela Bastidas?"

"José Gabriel's wife, executed along with him. She was a revolutionary leader as well. The Spanish destroyed her system, which held women in very high respect. Their oldest son and fifty-nine other family members and allies were also executed in a bloodbath in the Plaza de Armas of Cuzco."

"So, instead of preventing Antonio's radicalism, Pinochet pushed him into guerrilla warfare."

"Given the circumstances, it appears that way. Contrary to what many believe, revolutionaries aren't born. They're made by their circumstances. The real parents are hunger, humiliation, poverty, injustice, and tyranny. When tyranny is the law, rebellion is a right, as Simón Bolívar reminded us. The face of tyranny changes, but the human need for freedom never does."

"Do you believe that Pinochet's ideological war is still going on?"

Rafael nodded, adding, "A wall of secrecy still protects Operation Condor in spite of all of the declassified information made available by your country. Thousands of people who worked for Pinochet and his allies have never been duly prosecuted, including Pinochet, who was protected by people in high places until his death in 2006. Many are still drawing their pensions and dying peacefully or have been given legal or de facto amnesty. The historical truth has been truncated by political convenience. Nonetheless, we're the effect of the dead. An apology isn't necessary. The truth is."

"What about the United States?"

"Institutionalized child trafficking through foster care schemes still exists, and in your country, it's a $100-million-per-year business. I don't want to be unfair to those with good motives, but, given our history, we have to have a clinical eye when we examine any system. The same applies to your immigrant detention system because detention centers are run by private corporations that are more interested in money than justice or the rehabilitation of people."

"I understand that. I'm very aware of the failings of the system. After so many years, when I look back, I can tell you that Christian churches have been persecuted as well. Take the situation in El Salvador in the 1980s. Roman Catholics as well as non–Roman Catholic churches were persecuted."

Rafael nodded.

He continued. "The decade of the 1960s was a period of reform with Vatican II and leaders like General Velasco, but their reforms unleashed a right-wing counterattack in later decades."

"Yes," Rafael replied, "that period was part of the deep eclipse that Bolívar referred to, one that exercised an intentional objective to eradicate many groups by kidnapping their children. It wasn't child labor; it was genocide. The abduction of native children and women in Perú today speaks loudly."

"I think the military-industrial complex is behind that."

"Yes, we call it the gold road. Perú is the fifth-largest producer in the world. It has a strong illicit mining industry that's feeding jewelry and electronics producers."

"I assure you that my intention is to defend Isabel to the best of my ability," David offered. "I give you my word."

"Accepted."

"So, where is Antonio?"

Rafael took another bite of a bocado before he continued. He needed some fuel. "Actually, he's in Colombia." He described the roadside robbery by masked men and their interest in their cameras and recording equipment. "My manager in Turbaco went to his apartment in Cartagena, and neighbors told him that Antonio disappeared early the next morning when soldiers made an assault on his apartment."

David frowned.

"He's probably in Santa Marta."

"What is he doing in Santa Marta?"

CHAPTER 21

CHASING BOLÍVAR'S HEART

"Antonio is chasing Bolívar's heart," Rafael said. He shared the story about the existence of the letter and added, "Antonio is a pacifist and a poet. He wants to revolutionize the consciousness of his people by proving that Bolívar wanted his heart to be buried in Cuzco. It's his own way of rebuilding their spirit."

He added, "He went through the warrior stage of his life until he decided to survive and become an informant for the National Police of Perú. Then he married a Colombian and moved to Cartagena. By then, he decided to write a book on Bolívar, and that's when he met the historian from Santa Marta."

"Did the historian have the original letter?" David asked.

He shook his head. "The historian was searching for that original in the historical archives of Cartagena."

"Any trace?"

"No." He added the information that the historian had provided to Antonio, concluding, "The source of the information was a Dominican priest who had a copy of the letter. The historian just saw it. That's all I know. That's why the situation doesn't make sense unless we examine it from the perspective of our articles."

"But your articles are mostly about facts that are public knowledge."

"Most of them are."

"Seems to me that Antonio was able to join the Peruvian National Police because he was an asset to it."

"Yes. The MRTA was no longer considered a terrorist organization, and the police needed him because he could help them track down guerrillas who were still on the Most Wanted list."

"Who were they?"

"Those who had a record of serious violence."

"Which Antonio didn't have, correct?"

"Correct."

"So when he retired from DIRCOTE, he had paid his dues, even received a pension from the government," David speculated.

Rafael nodded.

"Until he began publishing articles that showed the ugly side of the counter-insurgency."

"In a way, our information war has been like a boomerang."

"But they aren't coming after you, Rafael."

He shook his head.

"So, why are they targeting him?"

He didn't answer.

"Have you made contact with Antonio recently?"

Again, Rafael shook his head.

They finished the bocados, ordered their respective meals, and continued the conversation. Rafael said, "Antonio was too young to participate in the Tupamaro movement in Uruguay. The Tupamaros were losing the struggle, especially when the US Office of Public Safety began to provide training and the armed struggle became really deadly. He moved to Argentina, where he started to work for the Revolutionary Coordinating Junta," but then, he had already witnessed the army's deadly death squads, mass arrests, and disappearances."

"I'm sure he wondered why he was kidnapped."

"Somehow, he knew that it was because of his lineage."

David nodded.

Rafael continued. "He became radicalized just like his ancestor José Gabriel Condorcanqui, and just like Miguel Hidalgo y Costilla, and just like Simón Bolívar, who articulated the desperation of Americans quite well. In all, it's a very complex situation, but Antonio's experiences are the same—a reaction to the enemy that lives within because we live in a world of apathy, blame, and misinformation while we cannibalize ourselves."

David emptied his cup of wine. He ate some of his *sombrero de Reyes* steak while Rafael completely ignored his meat lasagna.

Rafael was too involved with his story. "We're dealing with the exact same conditions today that existed when José Gabriel rebelled and when Miguel Hidalgo and Simón Bolívar declared independence from Spain, the same conditions. And that applies to the *norteamericanos* too. They don't have a clue about what's happening to all of us."

David answered. "Maybe they do know but aren't confronting the real facts."

"Or maybe," Rafael said, "we've been subjected to a campaign of silence that divides our hemisphere. This is happening from inside nations. You mentioned the military-industrial complex."

"What about it?" David replied, thinking of the chemtrails back home.

"We're bioengineering things that belong to nature, not to us—for instance, crops. We're doing it supposedly to make them drought-resistant and so on in the name of progress. Corporations are reengineering our living world, as Antonio says, without participating in that world. José Gabriel fought against the customs tax because it interfered with the exchange and sale of goods between Andean communities. To you, that would be taxation without representation. Worse, everything went to the king. What are we doing to protect our children and women against the slave trade or the kidnapping of young men outside Cuzco who are forced to work in the mines? Many are illegal mines. I can't point the finger at anyone—not yet— but silver, gold, and copper, for instance, that are used for electronic products create climate-damaging fumes and are exported without any interference by the state."

"If not forced, then the Indians are recruited by trickery. Going back more than two hundred years, why was Miguel Hidalgo so angry and why was Simón Bolívar so outraged? Antonio has more justification today for being a revolutionary. Antonio has seen the absolute savagery applied to his people, and yet he has opted out of the armed struggle."

"There are other ways to bring change," David said in a low voice. "Besides, I'm trying to build a defense for Isabel, and I don't see how Antonio's history is going to help."

"Correct." Rafael swallowed some lasagna and followed it with wine. "Here we are eating fine food in the middle of Guanajuato, the heart of the Mexican movement of independence, my friend, but this shouldn't keep us from looking at things bluntly. We've allowed others to design the 'truth,' so the historical record, both recent and distant, isn't the real record, starting with my own people, the Otomí, who still don't know where we came from although we know we're ancient, and continuing with Antonio's people, who are still waiting for their children to come back home. Fernando Condorcanqui is still buried in some grave in Madrid, waiting to be claimed by a country that pretends to be proud of its heritage. The last official survivor of Huayna Cápac, Juan Bautista, is still buried in La Recoleta in Buenos Aires."

David remained silent. Rafael needed to talk.

He added, "Antonio has a right to be upset. We're divided as a continent because we lay claim to foreign stories about ourselves, with codicils being burned or hijacked so that we would not know the true story. That's what Antonio sees."

"So, I repeat, why are they going after Antonio?"

"The letter by Bolívar was hijacked," Rafael argued. "The letter by Juan Bautista Condorcanqui was hijacked too. In the end, people always act in the interest of their own deluded economic or political agendas. Everything is short term, not long term. The last thing those in power or those seeking power want is to give any credibility to the real Americans, the native Andeans, or their resources."

"Why are they going after Antonio?" David asked again.

"Spain used our resources for several centuries. The United States and Europe are using our resources. Antonio is revealing how they're using those resources. Perú is the Latin American nation with the second-worst child slavery trade."

Rafael paused, adding, "Antonio and I decided to write a few articles about the insurgency of the 1970s and 1980s and about current conditions in the mining industry of Perú. We were assaulted by paramilitary enforcers who hid their faces, led by someone who doesn't have the courage to show himself, and that's the enemy we have to deal with. The enemy may be a shadow government similar to the one created by Pinochet, funded by private interests. We may blame the United States, which, of course, deserves all the blame for helping cutthroats like Videla and Pinochet and exporting corporate predators, but still, Antonio's quest isn't about blame. He knows more than you and I know about what the United States did or did not do. All he wants is to return the children to their homes, maybe not physically, but, as he likes to say, in the court of public opinion."

David nodded.

"The truth commissions haven't officially identified the culprits of the murders and disappearances in most cases."

"So, to return to the original question, do you think Pinochet prompted the kidnapping of Antonio and Isabel?"

"Of course."

"Do you believe that the same forces are manipulating them today?"

"Why did they hijack Bolívar's letter?" he responded. "Why is it important to hide something like that?"

"It's like destroying a mythological-genetic line of succession."

Rafael nodded, eating what was left of his meal.

"What's difficult to understand, though," David said, "is that the line was cut when they killed off and exiled everyone immediately connected to the Túpac Amaru line."

"It's difficult to understand but not impossible. It's as you said, my friend—they tried to destroy a very important mythological-genetic line of succession. For instance, the city of Troy was part of Greek and Roman mythology for centuries until the ruins of the city were discovered, supporting Homer's and Virgil's respective stories. Take this further. We discover that there are modern-day descendants of Helen and Paris who are seen as political threats to that region …"

"In this rational, modern world, I don't see that occurring."

Rafael smiled. "The Andean region of Latin America is different. The native Andean people believe their mythology in spite of efforts to erase it. Simón Bolívar believed in that mythology, not necessarily in the divine right of kings, but in the divine right of the people of the Americas to be themselves, to govern for the people, by the people." He sat back to take a sip of his wine.

"So," David offered, "as you yourself asked, why does the establishment want Antonio?"

"For the same sordid reasons they're going after him and not me. Therefore, it's not *just* the articles."

"What strategy should I follow?"

Rafael grinned. "If I were you, I wouldn't try to offer anything to Antonio because it's a trap."

David returned the grin. "I've reached that conclusion. As I mentioned, I may send Gloria to speak to him on behalf of Isabel. I'm not interested in serving the US government's agenda."

CHAPTER 22

THE POWER TO BE HEARD

Three days later, David turned on to the stone walkway that led to the stained-glass door of his building, flushed and sweaty from the daily run even though it was the first Monday in October. Stepping inside, he offered a fleeting smile to the receptionist as he walked across the foyer and canvassed the conference room. Everything was set up for the staff meeting in fifteen minutes, enough time to take a shower.

He had worked all weekend in an effort to lay the final groundwork for Isabel's case. He had called Rafael to thank him for his hospitality and to map out Gloria's possible trip to Turbaco to interview Antonio. Rafael was back in Venta Prieta and would leave in a couple of weeks for Turbaco.

Meanwhile, David's afternoon agenda brought everything together into a defense that would depend on Isabel. The interview would be videotaped. Representation by an attorney was allowed, but as a government-controlled and administrative rather than judicial event, it was limited to a legal statement at the end of the Isabel's interview. Of course, that wouldn't be enough to cover several centuries of history.

For this reason, the documentation in support of her asylum application, to be submitted later, was one hundred pages long. Dr.

Peltier's analysis of country conditions alone took twenty pages, and Dr. Warner's statement of Isabel's subjective fear and veracity took ten pages. The rest were used to stage a timeline of relevant historical events from 1780 to the present, which David would emphasize today. He was famous for setting up a record deserving of a space in the Library of Congress.

Before sitting at the head of the conference table, he glanced through the front window and took notice of the slow Monday traffic on Bishop Avenue. Three empty chairs surrounded the table, ready for those who would attend the meeting. The other chairs were against the wall. A collection of cupcakes and a pot of coffee sat in the center.

Elizabeth, the slim paralegal whose habit of squinting was a way of hiding her shyness, stepped into the meeting room. She was Jonathan's paralegal.

The rest stumbled in. Jonathan hadn't changed out of his golf clothes, and Gloria arrived ten minutes late, saying that she had had to make lunch for Isabel.

David, the systems theorist, was in charge. He stared at Gloria, who, as always, prepared herself for a lecture about Joseph Campbell or something similar. However, without hammering on too many details, David described his legal strategy, pausing occasionally for his usual cup of coffee.

The interview would be four days later. His legal arguments gave way to excitement. He read part of his cover letter to the asylum officer: "Ethnocide has pressured certain social groups to abandon their cultural-genetic identity and heritage. Mainstream institutions, guided by political or military or commercial objectives, or a combination thereof, have routinely pursued these de-Indianization efforts through the isolation and murder of Indian children as far north as Canada, where, in recent years, mass graves have been discovered, all the way south to Bolivia and Perú, where these children are routinely pushed into some kind of commercial bondage. Today, the child sex trade in Perú has reached alarming proportions; such ethnocide appears to be prompted by commercial objectives even though political objectives remain a part of the internal framework. This framework intends to stamp out indigenous persons such as Isabel Condorcanqui, who was kidnapped at the age of seventeen by agents of the state and forced into the slave trade." He paused.

Before Gloria could say anything, Jonathan, the most rational thinker of the staff, offered a concern. "What about Spain?" he asked. "There's a huge gap with Spain."

David nodded. "She was sent to Spain because the same networks exist over there."

"After so many centuries?"

"Isabel's main captor was a Spanish gentleman, apparently a judge, and her handlers were Peruvians. The chain of custody was never broken until they transferred her to Mexicans."

Gloria nodded.

David added, "A lawyer in Lima looked into police records and periodicals, and there was no indication of an investigation of her disappearance or her brother's kidnapping."

"We're talking about almost forty years, Mr. Levin," Jonathan answered. "Besides, maybe those events never happened."

"Well, her testimony is sufficient if it's credible, and I think it's credible."

Gloria didn't stay silent. "My goodness, why are you doing this?"

Jonathan shrugged. "Just arguing my point."

David nodded. "We have to set up distinctions that will present the big picture, including everything she said to the government. The government is going to compare her testimony with what she said initially. Everyone, even the government, is stuck in his own channel—Isabel on what happened to her, and the asylum officer on what he's supposed to do."

Jonathan wasn't convinced.

"Something awful *did* happen to her," Gloria said. "Why would she not talk about it? It's the foundation of her persecution case."

"You know how skeptical the system is, Mr. Levin," Jonathan argued.

David grinned. "So what are you trying to say? That it's fruitless?"

"Maybe."

"Are you saying that we should tell the asylum officer, 'Before I start talking to you, I should let you know that I already know that you're dishonest because you already know everything'?"

"Well ... no," Jonathan stammered.

"Kidnappings of native Andean women still happen today," Gloria stressed. "The conversation isn't just about her."

Everyone stared at her.

David turned to her. "Your conversation about the Diné doesn't belong just to the Diné people. It belongs to all Americans. As a nation, we can be joyful together or disjointed. We can't take away the trauma. The trauma that your father or mother and your ancestors went through isn't going to go away. You can't do anything about it. No one can undo something like that, whether it occurred intentionally or unintentionally. However, you have a responsibility to speak about your trail of tears, and we have an equal responsibility to listen to you."

"Isn't that what this asylum process is about, the blame game?" Jonathan asked.

Gloria frowned. Jonathan could be ridiculously rational.

David answered, "Isabel can tell her story, but she has to recognize the conversation she's embedded in so that she can motivate the asylum officer to take her side. No one can generate possibilities for himself except himself. Her fundamental conversation is that she's a Quechuan Condorcanqui, or Túpac Amaru, and that all governments have pursued a policy of not protecting her social group, her indigenous family. She needs to assert a commitment to provide the evidence, which she will do. She needs to declare her future, her new life as a Quechuan Condorcanqui. That's the key to her power to be heard. It's speaking her truth."

CHAPTER 23

CREDIBLE FEAR

A rush of adrenaline punched his chest when Antonio saw two cars and a pickup belonging to the National Police ahead of them. Wooden barricades blocked the road, keeping traffic at bay while drivers waited patiently for officers to perform a security check. Antonio glanced at Baralt. They were on the coastal road to Cartagena, a risk they had decided to take in order to pick up some money stashed away in Antonio's Jeep, still hidden in his friend's downtown hotel.

From there, they would proceed to Turbaco to wait for Rafael, whose input was crucial. However, it was possible that Rafael's hotel was under surveillance, a matter to be decided once he and Baralt scoped out the place. If so, they planned to wait for Rafael in Tenerife.

"*Tranquilo, amigo,*" Baralt said, noting to himself that Antonio's great adaptability to these situations was wearing thin. He adjusted his position behind the wheel, unflustered. They were fifteen minutes away from the ancient, walled city of Cartagena, and as the slow procession of traffic inched forward, he cocked his head. "We have to connect with our old soul, as some people say. If you can't do it, let it come to you, *hermano.*"

Antonio let out a laugh, aware of the stabbing pain in his head. He had no illusions of how these guys operated. The coastal road was the main artery linking Cartagena with Barranquilla, a favorite destination for security checks. His eyes adjusted to the officer's flashlight. It was focused on Baralt, who answered calmly.

"I'm Dr. Miguel Baralt. I'm heading to do some historical research in the archives." He handed over his *cédula* and a business card that displayed his credentials: membership in the Academy of History and the Bolivarian Society of the Magdalena as well as *doctor honoris* of the School of Social Sciences of Simón Bolívar University of Barranquilla.

The officer's flashlight darted to Antonio and then around the inside of the Renault. He directed his attention back to Baralt, saying, "And your companion?"

With subdued detachment, he said, "An amigo helping me with my project." After a slight pause, Baralt added, "You know, people are always trying to prove that Bolívar didn't die in Santa Marta."

The officer bristled. "Does your amigo have an identification card?"

"Of course he does."

Antonio gave him a small nod. "My cédula is in my knapsack in the trunk."

He took one step back. "Identify yourself!"

Antonio stiffened.

"*Señor*, please calm down!" Baralt exclaimed. "He's Esteban Perez Torices. Let's be civil, please. And with all due respect, his identification documents are in the trunk. I will vouch for that!"

He lowered the flashlight. "Do you live in Cartagena?"

"Yes," Antonio answered.

Someone called out the officer's name. The officer said, "Wait here," and walked toward a group of policemen.

In the meantime, Baralt heard a familiar voice. One of the supervisors was speaking to the officer. Baralt's head swung toward Antonio. "Looks like a supervisor recognized me."

"Do you know him?" Antonio asked.

"Yes. He was one of my students."

The officer spoke with his supervisor for several minutes and then waved the Renault through.

*****

The following morning, Isabel faced the asylum officer, who scrutinized her face under the fluorescent lights of his nondescript office, eventually letting his steely eyes settle on the forms in front of him. He was in his fifties. He had a strong Nordic face and dramatic blue eyes. He was massive and tall, a man who had a long record of pursuing law enforcement objectives. His demeanor, sharp nods and glances, concealed his thoughts. He betrayed not even a hint of skepticism regarding what was happening now.

His voice was calm and serious. "Okay, we've reviewed your background information," he said in Spanish, "and events after your arrival that led to your arrest." His broad shoulders hovered over the edge of the desk. He ignored Gloria, who was seated next to Isabel. He added, "Now, you have to establish that there's a significant possibility that your asylum application will be approved. Do you understand that once your parole is terminated you may be placed in expedited removal proceedings if you don't establish credible fear of persecution?"

It was difficult for Isabel to think, so she closed her eyes, followed her heart, and nodded at the officer.

"Do you understand what I just said?" he asked.

"Yes." She stroked the silver-turquoise necklace that Gloria had given her without glancing at Gloria, who had instructed her to maintain eye contact with the officer.

Isabel had repeated her story exactly as she had told it to ICE and to Gloria, beginning with her kidnapping in Cuzco, going through her years as a slave in Rio and Ceuta, and closing with her illegal crossing near Brownsville, Texas. She focused on her physical ordeal, occasionally eyeing the red light of the video camera on the wall.

The officer scribbled away. Finally, he looked up and said, "You haven't established a well-grounded fear of persecution by either country. You're pointing the finger at some underground, Mafia-like group that harassed you without showing that it had a government connection."

She let out a sigh and attempted to realign her thoughts. "Soldiers held me at gunpoint and pushed me into a car and took me to that jail."

"How do you know they were real soldiers?"

She raised her shoulders. "They were dressed like soldiers. They were armed with machine guns."

"What kind of car did they drive?" he asked.

"It was a regular car."

"Not an army car?"

"It was a car," she stated, shrugging. "They kidnapped me in broad daylight in the middle of Cuzco. No one interfered or tried to rescue me because they were soldiers."

"But they didn't take you to Lima, did they? Nor did they follow you to Spain."

"The soldiers delivered me to a jail. Later, they took me to civilians who were armed."

He sat back in his deep leathery chair, staring at her. "So how were you threatened?"

"How could I fight against a gun in my face?" Flustered, she glanced at the camera, ashamed of what she was about to say. "The soldiers took me to a jail where at least five of them raped me, one after the other." She started to sob. "They insulted me as an Indian whore; they insulted my family, my ancestors—José Gabriel and Juan Bautista Condorcanqui—and told me that they were planning to behead me."

Gloria remained still. David had instructed her to let everything fall in place.

Between sobs, Isabel continued. "At the end of this ordeal, a soldier put gunpowder in my insides between my legs and said that if I tried to run, I would blow up. I was too weak when he stuck his fingers in my insides, and then I was struck by a terrible headache for many days, vomiting, and terrible itching." She paused while sifting through what she had said.

"Did you see any of these soldiers for the next forty years?"

She shook her head. "Some of the men who transferred us to Lima showed up in Rio and Ceuta."

"What did they do?"

"They checked on me."

"Did they rape you?"

"No."

"So you weren't afraid of them," he said in a flat tone.

"Yes, I was. I always remembered the gunpowder and how it almost destroyed my insides. Besides, the Spanish head of the household beat me with a stick from time to time. He always called me *india bruta*. He was the one who continued to rape me."

The officer frowned. "Who was this man?"

She shrugged. "I gave you his name and address, didn't I?"

He nodded. "But who was he? What did he do for a living?"

"He was some kind of judge," she said.

"He worked for the Spanish government?"

"I think so."

He scribbled more notes and then continued. "We have information that your brother, Antonio Condorcanqui, joined the Tupamaros and later the MRTA. Do you know about these terrorist organizations?"

She tore her eyes away from him and glanced at Gloria for the first time. Gloria had not warned her about this. She could feel the bile in her throat. "Yes," she answered, smelling an ulterior agenda. "What does that have to do with me?"

"I have to establish whether you have persecuted other people."

She bristled. "How could I persecute anyone in my condition?"

"I don't know," he answered. "Maybe you sent money to Antonio."

"How could I do that, *señor oficial*, when they told me that he was dead? Besides, I was a slave, and slaves don't have any money. I couldn't look for him."

He frowned. "Have you had any association with a terrorist organization like the MRTA?"

"Why would I do something like that?"

"Don't answer me with a question. Just say yes or no."

Gloria stirred in her chair.

His tone hardened. "As I said, your brother was a terrorist. Do you know where he is?"

"No. I haven't seen or spoken with my brother in forty years." Ignoring the sharp, searing pain in her throat, she returned to her story, reliving the primal reaction of fear when the soldiers surrounded her as tightly packed groups of pedestrians watched from the sidewalks. Before they applied the chloroform, they tormented her and cursed her until she relented and shouted the whereabouts of Antonio.

"So you told them where to find him?"

She remained silent.

"Answer me. You told them where they could kidnap him?"

Whimpers gave way to loud sobs. She said yes in a hollow voice. Spurred by the guilt of what she had done, she cradled her face in her hands, forcing Gloria to bolt out of her chair to offer consolation. However, as soon as she placed her hands on her right shoulder, Isabel stood up, took one step forward, and fainted.

*****

Antonio and Baralt carefully canvassed the road ahead of them. They were out of the chaotic bustle of Cartagena, heading toward Rafael's oasis. They had picked up the stashed cash the previous night and left as soon as they had breakfast in the morning. Weariness lined their faces even though they were convinced that some kind of divine intervention had protected them from a National Police assault the night before. Although nervous, they settled into the task of delivering a copy of Bolívar's letter to Rafael while they watched for some sign of suspicious activity along the road. Antonio briefly described the eco-hotel's charms as Baralt drove.

Traveling with Baralt was like being in one of his classrooms. The conversation always turned into a history lesson of some kind. Baralt was addicted to the history of the region.

"They accused Bolívar of being a tyrant," he offered.

"He was eaten up by his children," Antonio said.

"In reality, he was a product of the times, like children complaining about the patriarch when, in reality, he was nurturing them into adulthood."

"He was very aware of their cynicism. Actually, the people of Bogotá didn't believe in anything. 'Superficial' is what he called us. The people of Cartagena didn't help him either, and they did it without blinking."

Baralt let out a sigh, adding, "He was swimming against a current filled with cynicism even though he had the vision we needed."

"Well, he wasn't a politician."

"Bolívar was a military man."

"Yes, he was an excellent strategist," Antonio acknowledged. "He knew that the native Andean community truly appreciated what he did for us." His mind recalled the letter that his ancestral grandfather had written to Bolívar. He knew it by memory:

> I have survived to the age of eighty-six, despite great hardships and having been in danger of losing my life, to see consummated the great and always just struggle that will place us in the full enjoyment of our rights and liberty. This was the aim of Don José Gabriel Túpac Amaru, my venerated and affectionate brother and martyr of the Peruvian Empire, whose blood was the plow which prepared that soil to bring forth the best fruits; [but it was left to] the Great Bolívar to harvest them with his valiant and generous hands. Juan Bautista Túpac Amaru.

Baralt continued. "Reasons existed for not answering your grandfather's letter. When Bolívar returned to Bogotá in late 1826,

Santander opposed his idea of a federation of the Andes. Only a few greeted his return, unlike previous times. Actually, I believe that Bolívar saved what was left of Juan Bautista's life."

Antonio waved at him to slow down. Nothing appeared out of place. "There's an abandoned house on the left five minutes away. Let's go there."

Baralt nodded.

He added, "Park on the side behind a grove of trees. They will hide the vehicle."

"What do you have in mind?"

"If I remember things right, there's a hiking trail behind the house that leads to the property."

As he expected, a modest, concrete, one-story house stood a few yards from the road, gutted by fire as a result of intense army fighting with the drug cartel lord whose hacienda now belonged to Rafael.

Antonio and Baralt stepped out of the Renault and cut through the tropical vegetation until they detected a trail that led them to the massive ten-foot wall around Rafael's hotel. The area surrounding the wall was still accessible, though riddled by trails. A few men and women had used this disorganized patchwork of paths fed by water streams, ancient trees, and tropical forest for their guerrilla or drug-related missions.

They reached a rough wooden door that shuddered on its rusted hinges when Antonio pulled it open. He took a hesitant step and leaned forward. The sound of splashing water came from the right, a natural spring on this side of the hacienda. As soon as he moved through the door, the tip of a machete appeared in front of him. He glanced up. It was José, staring at him.

"Señor Antonio, what are you doing here?" a startled José asked.

"Looking for Rafael," he said as José assisted him with his knapsack. He turned around and introduced Dr. Baralt. "Is he here?"

"I'm expecting him any day now," José answered, moving toward the house. He didn't ask why Antonio had used the hiking trail. He didn't have to.

"Do you have any guests?" Antonio asked.

He shook his head. "We're expecting a group from Canada tomorrow." He led them to the kitchen where Amalia was preparing lunch. They sat down at the table while Amalia, who wasn't a talkative person, served them coffee in silence.

"You can stay here and wait for Señor Rafael," José offered.

"We have a few errands to do," Antonio answered, "so just tell him to contact our old friend in Tenerife."

CHAPTER 24

THE TRIP

Gloria slumped down into the leather chair in front of David's desk, exhausted. She had left Isabel with one of her daughters at home and hurried to the office for a debriefing with David. After describing what had taken place in the credible fear interview, she gauged nothing from his demeanor except for a wistful calm about him. He leaned against the back of his chair and silently looked back at her as if waiting for questions to settle in his head.

Gloria was obviously distraught. "I didn't get an opportunity to close with an argument," she said. "Isabel needed to get out of there."

"Did you request another interview?" he asked.

"Yes, but the officer said that he had enough information with your cover letter and Dr. Warner's report and all of the other documents we provided."

David remained silent.

Gloria frowned. "I can't wrap my head around all the questions he asked about Antonio. I mean, it was as if he was more interested in Antonio."

"Did he ask where Antonio was?"

She nodded. "Isabel told him she didn't know, that she hadn't spoken with him in forty years."

"Did the officer acknowledge that the kidnappers were paramilitary troops?"

"No, he referred to them as an underground Mafia network. I mean, Isabel was a seventeen-year-old girl. How would she know whether they were soldiers or paramilitary troops?"

"How did she describe them?"

"Isabel told him that they looked like soldiers." She stared at him, wondering why he was pretending to find the truth when there was no such thing. "Mr. Levin, what are we going to do?"

He stood up, walked to the window facing the parking lot below, and glanced at Jonathan and the paralegals leaving for the day. Without turning, he said, "Isabel is the victim of a conspiracy called programmatic genocide that goes back centuries in which institutions have colluded across geographic boundaries. They're trying to cover up something that's going on now; that's why they're interested in Antonio. He's become a liability."

"Yes, the Franco and the Dirty War connection with child trafficking, and the Christian Indian Residential School connection that reprogrammed my people, except that Antonio and Isabel were too old to be reprogrammed."

David turned around. "And Antonio got away. In any event, Antonio and Isabel still pose a threat to those who are protecting their assets. The asset may be ideological or something material like the gold that's being mined in Perú. Remember that it's what *they* perceive as a threat. So, would you be willing to travel to Colombia to interview Antonio?"

"What for? He'll never agree to come to the United States."

He returned to his chair. "Maybe he'll give us a sworn statement. He has some credibility. Remember, chasing porcupine is about making the right choices."

She smiled. "What do you have in mind, Mr. Levin?"

"Rafael Aguilar can get us a meeting with Antonio."

"What am I supposed to do?"

"Antonio needs to know about Isabel before he returns to Perú."

"Why does he want to go back?" she asked.

"He has a letter that he wants to take to Cuzco."

She waited for more information.

David added, "Antonio was able to locate a copy of a letter in which Bolívar donated his heart to the people of Cuzco. The letter appears to be legitimate. Antonio wants to deliver it to the region of Cuzco."

"But is he willing to cooperate with us? I mean, Isabel is here and he's over there."

David leaned forward over the edge of his desk. "You like to say that Jonathan can be infuriatingly rational."

"Am I doing that?" she asked.

He didn't answer her question. "As I said, you can draw up a statement in which he confirms that he was kidnapped by paramilitary troops. Antonio eventually tracked down Isabel when he was with DIRCOTE and located her in Ceuta, further confirming her story. He can also attest to the fact that she and he are descendants of José Gabriel Condorcanqui, Túpac Amaru II."

"Who told you that?"

"Rafael Aguilar."

"Do we have time to submit that statement to the government?" she asked.

"It's never too late to submit evidence that wasn't available at the credible fear interview."

"When do you want me to go?"

"Let me line things up with Rafael."

CHAPTER 25

THE LAW OF RECIPROCITY

Rafael was eagerly waiting for Gloria when she stepped out through the door of airport customs. He had arrived in Cartagena and rented a car over a week earlier without alerting his staff, and he had stayed in a downtown hotel until Gloria arrived. Security was his priority.

As soon as they met, he was jolted by her presence even though she wore a simple black linen dress without any jewelry. Her long black hair was appropriately pulled back and braided together with small turquoise beads to lessen the hot, humid climate's assault on her senses. The intense heat that hovered over the city was occasionally broken by showers, but those were soon to end at the beginning of December, or in two weeks.

He opted to describe the history of the region on their twenty-minute drive to Turbaco while she quietly absorbed the roadside landscape and occasionally nodded at him.

"This is an agricultural and cattle region," he said, pointing at the cattle that brooded in unison under a tree.

"Why did you decide to settle in Turbaco?" she asked.

"Oddly enough, a famous countryman of mine settled in Turbaco around 1850, Antonio Lopez de Santa Anna."

"*The* Santa Anna of the Texas-Mexico War?"

He laughed. "Yes, the same Santa Anna whose troops fought against your people at the Alamo. A couple of years after he was forced into exile, he came here and did a lot for the town—built a cemetery and the Alcaldía and gave books to the local library. A few of his descendants are buried here."

She mulled over the information in silence.

"Anyway, it was one of the factors that influenced me," he said. "In fact, Turbaco has attracted other famous people, among them Simón Bolívar, who spent some time here trying to get his health back before leaving for Europe."

"He died in Colombia, right?"

"He did. The thermal water treatments helped him, but, still, he was too ill for a trip across the Atlantic, so he headed to Soledad and later, to Santa Marta."

"Was Santa Anna from your part of Mexico?"

"No, from Xalapa, Veracruz, and I'm from Venta Prieta in the state of Hidalgo, four hours away. There's a Mexican-Jewish community like mine in the city of Veracruz, an interesting coincidence, just like the fact that Santa Anna was born eleven years after Bolívar."

"He was a contemporary."

"He became president of Mexico three years after Bolívar died. He had a different mission because he fought against the movement of independence until he joined it, so he wasn't a Miguel Hidalgo or a Simón Bolívar. He wasn't sympathetic to our indigenous people either. Nonetheless, he governed Mexico for over two decades."

"So how do you manage your busy life?" she asked.

"Writing is a quiet exercise," he answered, "and I can do it while I'm here. When I travel, it's for interviews or research or to visit my family. What about you?"

"It's my first trip to Colombia. In fact, the only other country I've visited is Mexico."

He swung the car through an arched portal with an open wrought-iron gate and pulled up to his two-level stucco hotel. From the car, she admired the woodlands that flanked the building. He opened the door for her. "There's a courtyard in the center of the house and guest rooms around it. I'm sure you'll like your room," he said with pride while he relished the thought of dining with her that night. He was met by José, who took their bags to their respective rooms on the second floor.

After Rafael escorted her to her room, he joined José and Amalia in the kitchen. He opted not to say that he and Antonio had been already in touch through the classifieds of *El Heraldo*, where Rafael left his new cell phone number to Inti. The opportunity arose when Rafael received the expected call. Antonio had called him from Tenerife, mentioning his visit to the hotel. They scheduled a meeting at the Manga Island yacht club for tomorrow. Rafael said nothing about Gloria, the best way to handle this unpredictable situation.

He swirled some milk in his coffee and waited for José's information.

"Antonio was here," José said. "He came through the secret hiking trail. Said to contact an old friend in Tenerife if you need to see him. He came with Dr. Baralt."

Rafael didn't answer.

"Do you know who he is?"

"Yes." He sipped his coffee slowly and then asked, "Has anyone else asked for me?"

"Your accountant."

"Any indication that we're being watched?"

José shook his head. "Is there anything you want me to do?" he asked him.

"How many guests do we have?"

"Three couples from Canada."

"We should have some music," he answered. "Call the musicians."

In the meantime, Gloria unlocked the balcony door and stepped out to absorb the beauty of the land. Between an orange sky and green tropical trees on a hill, clear water flowed through the forest. She could hear the water. The place emitted a soft breeze with its own perfume, and although humid, something special graced the air. Things had a way of being connected—for instance, the sparks of fireflies gliding through the darkness below the trees in a magical dance with the holy people of this place. She didn't need to see the holy people to know that they were there and were related to the guardians of the four mountains and four rivers where her people were created. She turned around, extracted a simple necklace with turquoise beads, and placed it around her neck. Turquoise was an ancient protective amulet prized by not only the Navajo but also by the Egyptians. The beads gave her energy. Mother Power is what she called it.

At seven in the evening, dinner began when four men with three guitars and a set of maracas offered ballads while cocktails were served. When they sang "Si nos dejan" by Alfredo Jimenez, Rafael sprang up and joined the group.

"Si nos dejan, nos vamos a querer toda la vida," he sang, directing his attention to Gloria. "Si nos dejan, nos vamos a vivir a un mundo nuevo."

He didn't take his eyes off her and followed with more Mexican ballads until they settled into a typical Colombian meal.

The admiration was mutual. "I never expected you to sing so well," she said softly.

He grinned, his gaze caressing her face. "It's one of the benefits of having Mexican genes."

She paused for a breath and paused again. When she retired to her room, she tried to control her emotions, turning in her bed frequently as she listened to the chatter in her head. Doubts inspired by her widowhood subsided as soon as she realized that she was feeling guilty, and then she fell asleep.

*****

Early the next morning, before the rest of the guests were up, Gloria enjoyed an upscale rural breakfast served in the kiosk in the company of Rafael, who flattered her with more compliments.

She didn't ask where they were going, but he told her anyway. "We're headed to Manga Island." He glanced at her. "I'm not sure about this location, but those are Antonio's instructions."

"Is it dangerous?"

He nodded. "It's the mouth of the wolf. No one expects him to take this risk."

When they walked up to the old fort and reached the gate, Jorge, who was waiting for them, walked over, prepared for a handshake. It was eight o'clock in the morning. The restaurant was empty except for a cleaning crew.

"Good to see you," he said. "Antonio is at the edge of the water. Most employees will begin to arrive in an hour or so. We have time."

They followed him to the designated place.

Antonio and Baralt were waiting. After the introductions, they sat down. The look on Antonio's face made it obvious that he was wondering why Gloria was there. She, in turn, studied his square forehead, high cheekbones, and black eyes, which were identical to Isabel's. His nose was different, longer and hooked, compared to hers. He was a medium-boned man, unlike Baralt, whose build was smaller and bony. She liked Baralt's scholarly looking gray hair.

Rafael broke the ice. "This is Gloria. She's from the United States, and she brings a message from your sister, Isabel."

Antonio's face revealed a deep unease. He stirred in his chair. "She's dead," he said in a hardened tone as he looked away.

Gloria stepped in. "I come here with a message of peace from your sister, Isabel Condorcanqui Túpac Amaru. I'm her attorney."

His muscles tightened. His voice cut through the air. "Why does she need an attorney?"

"She's in trouble with the government of the United States, Mr. Condorcanqui. I need to speak with you in private. You're her only surviving blood relative."

Suddenly he stood up. "Very well. Follow me." He walked fast toward the old canons facing the bay. When they reached the seawall, he asked her to sit down, and he followed suit. The morning sunlight competed with the traffic in the bay. They stared at each other for a few seconds until she started speaking. She told him about Isabel's trials, including the terror she went through when arrested and raped by agents of a shadow government that was still causing havoc in her life.

A deep anger ran through his body. "Did she tell you what she did?" he asked in an acid tone.

"Yes."

"How dare she try to make contact after so many years!" he snapped.

"She was told that you were killed while trying to escape from your kidnappers."

He said nothing.

"Please understand how devastating that was."

He remained silent.

"She was a slave. She was brutally beaten and humiliated, and she was watched. She was also told that her parents and her sister died in a car accident. I myself don't blame her."

His eyes were locked on her face. "When did she find out that I was alive?"

"Months ago. They told her that they would help her find you if she went to the United States." She added, "Please remember what happened to your ancestors."

He bristled. "My ancestors," he said in an icy voice, "never betrayed each other."

She took in his words, nodded, and stood up. Facing him, she answered, "Well, it's obvious that you've forgotten that your grandfather, Juan Bautista, denied his relationship to José Gabriel Condorcanqui in 1781 to save his skin."

He liked her firepower. "You know our history well."

"And you've been an informant for the National Police of Perú."

"What are you implying?"

"That you should be the last one to throw salt on Isabel's integrity."

His head turned away.

"Isabel said that she rides on the waves of the moon and that ayni isn't for sale, so she hasn't given up on you."

"What are you proposing?" he asked.

"We're not proposing anything. We don't represent the government of the United States, and besides, we don't have all of the facts. However, they've offered you a U visa, which means that you could travel to the United States as a witness against top officials of the Colombian and Peruvian governments who are implicated in slave trafficking in our country. However, Mr. Levin and I suspect that they're using Isabel to reel you in. It's also possible that someone wants you locked away because your articles are embarrassing a few powerful sectors that don't want this publicity."

He glanced at the ground. "What's going to happen to Isabel?"

"I don't know. If she gets asylum, she'll probably remain in the United States. If she gets deported to Perú or Spain, she runs the risk of being either killed or kidnapped."

"But they're after me," he argued.

She shook her head. "The plain facts are that they're going after your family. Forty years ago, you were a boy of fourteen years. No one cared or knew about you, yet the kidnappings occurred. Your parents and sister were killed in a car accident a year later. Those events weren't accidental. Isabel's arrival in the United States wasn't accidental either. The facts speak for themselves."

Slowly, an emotional storm swept through him, causing his breath to erupt short and fast and forcing him to raise his hands to hide his face. He bent over. Gloria sat down again and edged over to him so that her words could be heard clearly. "I'm an Indian like you. I'm the last person to remind you of Inti and Quilla. We understand this relationship. We also understand that you and Isabel have a duty to stay alive, together, so that the divine can continue manifesting through you. To us, it's a partnership. You have a position of responsibility."

She scrutinized the side of his face, still covered by his hands, and continued. "Your family manifests Inti and Quilla. The source is living through you. You're part of a continent with a sacred inheritance bombarded by foreign values that don't understand ayni. But ayni goes on, not because we have any control over it but because it is what it is. Nothing exists in a vacuum. You know that. Isabel knows that, and I know that."

He glanced around to be sure that no one was watching them.

She imagined what his life must have been like since the kidnapping. His family had been brutally persecuted. From that moment on, her mind began to have thoughts about bringing Isabel back home; however, she reminded herself of David's words: "Believe nothing and believe everything."

She continued. "Do you know what my children often say to me?"

He glanced at her and waited.

"That I'm a lecturing machine." She laughed, enjoying this light moment. "Isn't that what I'm supposed to be?"

He nodded.

"Life is always interrupted by the most banal things. So, I spend most of my time lecturing my children about what's important. Things like family, love, friends, compassion, unity. I was married to a Mexican man who prayed to the Virgin of Guadalupe, also known as Tonantzin. To us, Tonantzin is ShimáNahasdzáán, and when I met Isabel, I learned about Pachamama. There are thousands of indigenous groups in the Americas who have a relationship with the same mother. We speak in different dialects and languages and follow different customs without interrupting what's inherent in all of us. No one can separate Inti from Quilla. No one can divide ShimáNahasdzáán from Pachamama."

Emotionally battered, he concentrated his gaze on the ground. He wasn't a man to be pounded by emotions, yet he couldn't fall back on what was part of his old repertoire, a logical detachment that had saved his life on many occasions. He started to sob loudly.

She didn't rush to comfort him. After several minutes, she offered, "As an attorney, I have to follow conventions of the modern world. Almost everyone expects me to get on an airplane to Bogotá, help you to apply for a U visa at the consulate, and bring you to the United States. This is a project outside of my inner landscape. It's a spiritual challenge for me. However, I have figured out things."

He didn't have much to say. Isabel was his family.

She took command of the opportunity. "I'm returning home in a few days and will deliver your decision to Isabel."

"In a few days, I'll be leaving for Cuzco," he said suddenly.

"You're taking a tremendous risk."

"I must visit some friends. One of them is Apu, the sacred perpetual mountain. Do you know why I need to visit Apu?"

She shook her head.

"To remind myself that life is a pilgrimage." He added, "I must remind myself that there are others who need help. All the living hearts come together at Apu Qoyllur Rit'i, and all the people who walk this journey are chosen, predisposed to regenerate Father Mountain and Mother Earth, to give them light. In return, we will receive their blessings. I will take Bolívar's letter and speak about it."

"Why is it so important?"

"Bolívar's heart isn't physical anymore. It's the message. Bolívar gave us a voice. I don't have descendants, but the stars are my sisters, the lakes are my grandparents, the hills and mountains are my protectors, so I must go to Apu to ask for his blessings. It's no mystery. We're all related. We have the same ancestors. Bolívar invoked Atahualpa, recognizing the unbearable torment and humiliation inflicted upon our people by the Spanish because he was aware that we're related. Bolívar is a member of our family."

CHAPTER 26

DIVINE INTERVENTION

Gloria awakened in Rafael's arms the following morning, clothes and sheets bunched up on the polished dark red tile floor next to the bed. The smell of rain in the breeze wafted in through the open balcony, as if feeding the power of her womb to create new beginnings. She let out a deep, long sigh, aware that she was making up for several lost lifetimes. She could remain here in Turbaco forever.

Dawn was drifting in, so she sat up until Rafael pulled her back to him and locked his arms around her. His eyes maneuvered a smile. "We have all the time in the world," he whispered, landing an exquisite kiss on her lips. She relaxed. The side of this lifetime had no limitations. Their lovemaking was slow compared to the fast and furious pace of the previous night. They were like two old and wise souls making up for lost time.

By midmorning, she raised her head from his chest and caressed his face with one hand while the other landed over his mouth as he was about to say something. She moved closer and bit his lower lip, whispering, "As you said yesterday, we're going to love each other for the rest of our lives. Come with me, my love ..."

"I never thought that I would find you here," he said, grabbing her shoulders.

"I came to take you home," she said with a seductive smile.

He repeated a few of the lyrics he had sung the day before. "Y ahi, juntitos los dos, cerquita de Dios, será lo que soñamos."

She moved her naked body toward the bathroom and studied her reflection in the wall mirror, reminding herself of what David had said about things being worked out on another level. His words raced through her mind: "The community is no longer a town or a country or even a region. Today, the community is the planet."

She never expected to fall in love again with anyone, especially not in a country besides her own, but events had brought her together with Rafael in Colombia, another Mexican like Juan. ShimáNahasdzáán and Tonantzin and Pachamama were watching over her.

*****

At noon, David sprinted out through the front door of his office and followed his usual jogging route toward the arts district, where he had a lunch meeting in twenty minutes. Bishop Avenue was calm—no historic tours in sight. Dallas deliberately discouraged almost everything tied to its past, especially what it considered its toxic past, or toxic art, for that matter. The garden pink flamingos that turned orange with each sunset were now the target of neighborhood watch groups concerned with socially responsible art, whatever that meant.

It was a mystery how human civilization had lasted this long given its insane priorities. Nuclear proliferation. Killing the Amazon. Geoengineering, like the metals that left chemical fumes in our air space to modify sun rays and rain patterns. The chemtrails' debris was increasingly associated with brain disorders such as Alzheimer's.

However, he had other matters to worry about. He was thinking of his telephone conversation with Gloria, who was scheduled to arrive the following evening. Her report had been cryptic. "I spoke with Antonio."

"Did he sign a sworn statement?" he asked.

"Yes."

"Good. His statement will strengthen the asylum."

"I'll scan it and send it by e-mail before packing it. Just a precaution."

"How is he doing?"

"Things are being worked out on another level. Antonio is going to his homeland for the Apu Qoyllur Rit'i. He's taking Bolívar's letter."

"Duly noted."

"We'll talk tomorrow."

He crossed the street and ended up in front of the Spanish cuisine café, wondering why Agent Mark Gardner didn't want to meet him at the law office. He entered the café and asked for a table and some Tempranillo wine while he continued to mull over the crisis point of the world that some called our nature deficit disorder. Some wine would help him to accept the consequences.

As soon as the waiter left, a stocky man in civilian clothes whose blond hair and blue eyes softened his implacable gaze walked in and asked for him. Of medium height, stocky but athletic with broad shoulders, Agent Gardner stood rigidly, almost sternly, like a man twice his age. He strode toward David in a way that instinctively reminded David of all government officials.

ICE Agent Mark Gardner introduced himself and sat down. He ordered a cup of coffee.

"Hmm," David said while taking note of his civilian clothes—a cotton shirt under an open wool vest and faded jeans. He had met many FBI, DEA, ICE, CBT, and INS agents, to name a few, but never in this informal setting. He was glad that he was drinking this Tempranillo. "Care for some tapas?" he asked. "The oxtail and *papas bravas* are excellent."

Agent Gardner shook his head.

"Well, I'm going to order some," he said. "Food is our way of connecting with the world, don't you think?"

He nodded.

"Have we met before?"

"No, not directly" he said. "I met your attorney, Gloria García, at the hospital. I was the officer guarding Isabel Condorcanqui. I ran into them again at the credible fear interview."

"Ah, so, did you conduct the interview?"

"No, sir. I escorted them to the interviewer."

"Were you present at the interview?"

He shook his head. "But I watched the videotape after it took place."

David ordered his tapas and another glass of wine. The conversation was getting interesting. He didn't know whether to become furious or to enjoy the mystery. He opted for the latter.

"I'm here in my personal capacity, Mr. Levin, and I have a few things to communicate to you. I know that I'm the last person you can trust, but I'm not here to win your trust. You can take my information or just throw it out the window."

He tapped the table. "Go on."

"You've been around for a long time, and my colleagues respect you. They say that your integrity is beyond reproach, something that I took into consideration when I decided to speak to you. I also believe that nothing effectively manages the government except the people."

"Well said, son."

"I'm not only an American citizen but a Choctaw."

"You don't look like a Choctaw."

He grinned and nodded. "I'm a card-carrying Choctaw from Hugo, Oklahoma."

"Do you have the card with you?"

He frowned. "No. My mother has it. She's a pure Choctaw. She guards it with her life. My father is white."

"Ah. So how can you prove it to me?"

"Other than sending you a copy later, I can show you my marks."

"Marks?"

"Yes. Sundance."

"I didn't know that Choctaws did Sundance."

He unbuttoned the top of his cotton shirt and bared his pectoral piercing marks, which clearly revealed that he had participated in Sundance. The Western world knew only a fraction about the Lakota ceremony of life and rebirth, but David knew enough to realize that he could be telling the truth.

The tapas were served. "Are you sure you don't want any?" David asked.

He shook his head. "I was there in the hospital, and I witnessed several of Isabel's episodes. The videotape reveals the same trauma." After a pause, he added, "The government plans to deny that she has shown any credible fear of persecution, Mr. Levin, and plans to remove her to Spain, which is in the process of accepting her return."

"Just like Fernando Condorcanqui," David said, feeling his jaw tighten.

"Who?"

"An ancestor," he answered, "who's buried in Madrid. He never got back to Perú."

He nodded.

"What about her brother, Antonio?"

He stirred in his chair. "They're using Isabel as a pawn. The plan to deny her asylum claim."

"How soon?"

"Soon."

"You know I can delay things," David said.

"Yes."

"I don't think Antonio is going to accept the deal, Agent Gardner."

"I understand."

"He won't come to the United States."

He nodded.

"So," David said, leaning forward, "what's going on? Why are they interested in a washed-out former urban guerrilla fighter who turned government informant?"

He hunched his shoulders. "I believe it has to do with the mining industry of Perú, which feeds us many metals that are crucial to several industries. Antonio's articles are interfering with this agenda."

"Why not prosecute him in Perú? Why go through all this nonsense?"

"He worked for DIRCOTE. He can compromise some people in the government."

"Is that it? He knows too much?"

"Yes. As a former MRTA member, he was pardoned by the government of Perú. That's not the case with us. We can still press charges against him for destroying US property and attacking our agents."

"Do you believe that we would take that risk? Operation Condor is an embarrassment."

He nodded. "He could do some damage. However, I don't think that matters."

"Go on."

"Millions of dollars are tied up with precious metals that are mined and exported. They're using our Indian men, children, and women as laborers."

"They're Peruvians."

"Not just Peruvians. They're Native Americans. They're my people." He stood up.

David glanced at him. "Did Karl Segal put you up to this?"

He didn't answer the question. "I have to do what's right, Mr. Levin."

As soon as David finished his lunch and paid the bill, he walked back to his office without rushing to give himself enough time to think about his next move. Once he reached his desk, which was overflowing with legal documents he was reviewing, he stared ahead. Karl Segal fed off the political garbage that always walked into his office under the flag of good conscience; however, it was possible that he couldn't justify pimping himself for a special interest group this time. Too much of that was going on. Politicians in Washington DC, for instance, were trying to grab sacred Apache land in Arizona for the benefit of the mining industry.

Suddenly he thought of his friend, Joseph Gomez. He used his land line to call Joseph, an ex-US Marine Vietnam veteran who was also a Lipan Mescalero Apache in New Mexico.

Joseph believed in migration rather than immigration given that the Apache people, who inhabited a region that stretched from San

Luis Potosí, Mexico, into the United States had a difficult time with borders. They had migrated back and forth for thousands of years.

When Joseph answered the phone, he was glad to hear that David Levin was interested in Apu Qoyllur Rit'i. "Didn't expect you to go Indian on me," Joseph said with a laugh.

"Well, I am. I suddenly remembered that you did this pilgrimage from time to time. How long does it take?"

"Well, a group of cars drives up to the border and joins another caravan of cars …"

"On the other side?"

"Yes. We have brothers and sisters waiting for us who drive us to the next border until we reach the Sinakara Valley of Perú. So, to answer your question, sometimes it takes the first three weeks of May, sometimes four weeks, depending on the weather, volcanoes, earthquakes, tsunamis, and so on that afflict that part of the world." He paused. "But we have always reached our destination, brother. It's an important event for the indigenous people of Perú and Bolivia."

"How many attend it?"

"About sixty to one-hundred thousand people. Care to tell me how you were struck by Qoyllur Rit'i? It's not an easy trip."

"Guess I'm looking for trouble." There was a hint of humor in his voice.

Joseph laughed. "At our age, we should always look for trouble."

"Exactly. When are you leaving?"

"Monday, May 4. Join us at sunrise at my home."

"Care if I bring one of my attorneys, Gloria Dolii García?"

"Is she a Native American?"

"Yes, from Magdalena, New Mexico."

"Navajo?"

"Correct."

"Care if a client of mine joins your pilgrimage?"

"Should I ask any questions?"

"No."

"No problem. I'll see you in May."

CHAPTER 27

POMACANCHI

Rafael Aguilar and David Levin were the first ones to arrive at the designated meeting place on a road overlooking the Lagoon of Pomacanchi, named after the town nestled in the Peruvian highlands southeast of Cuzco. They had driven over one and a half hours after a quiet breakfast in their hotel near the Plaza de Armas.

At that time, Rafael told David of his intention to propose to Gloria as soon as he returned to Turbaco. He also updated David on Isabel's arrival in Mahuayani on May 25 in the company of Joseph Gomez plus five women and sixteen men from different northern tribes. Antonio was waiting for them.

As eloquent as Rafael could be, the meeting had stretched everyone toward a level of being that couldn't be conveyed easily. "The meeting was like a communal rebirthing," he explained. "It stretched all of us. A clear, powerful energy came from beneath the ground and joined another from above, so there was no opportunity for Antonio and Isabel to react to each other except to hug each other for a long time. A bolt of the divine hit each of us. Enormous strength came from admitting that the universe is a living organism. Mountains and skies joined together and interacted with us. As soon as we recovered from the bolt of energy, we picked up our things and started the hike to Apu Ausangate's valley in silence."

David listened quietly.

"In any event, I'll write about it someday," he said with a slight smile while he scanned the lagoon and surrounding landscape. Traffic was slow at this time of the day. He was leaning against the rented car, parked on the inside lane of the road.

Rafael had left the group the previous day in order to join David in Cuzco.

"So," David asked, "what's in store for Antonio and Isabel? They're probably on everyone's lookout list."

"They're going underground," Rafael answered. "They'll probably go to Bolivia, which offers a friendlier environment."

His eyes adjusted to the increasing intensity of daylight. The high altitude was exhausting, so he pulled a few coca leaves from his jacket and offered some to David, whose eyes soon shifted from the mountains that skirted the lagoon to the road toward Joseph, who was already walking toward Rafael's rented car. Rafael shook Joseph's hand.

A straw hat from central Mexico covered Joseph's head. He was wearing his favorite T-shirt, which showed a portrait of four Apache warriors armed with rifles under the message, "Homeland Security, Fighting Terrorism Since 1492." He and David were members of a powerful generation following the conventions of the modern world yet working outside of those conventions. In spite of their ethnic and religious differences, both understood the Maya greeting, "In Lakesh," which meant "I'm another you," a message that when we harm someone else, we harm ourselves. Because of them, members of seven indigenous nations from North and Central America delivered Isabel Condorcanqui to her brother, Antonio, in Mahuayani, Perú.

"Do you think anyone here understands your message?" Rafael asked Joseph.

He grinned. For someone who always said that he was nineteen thousand years old, his fighting spirit never faltered. "Well, I brought more T-shirts with other messages in case they miss this one."

As soon as Isabel stepped out of Joseph's car, she ran up to David and embraced him, placing her head against his chest while he stroked her head. She had lived through so much. "You're my father, Mr. David," she said again and again, with tears streaming down her cheeks. She had used Gloria's passport to cross each border between the United States and Perú. She was instructed to destroy it once she reached Perú.

She looked stunning in her Quechuan dress. She was wearing a colorful wool jacket with multicolored beads woven into the front panels over a yellow sweater. Her skirt had layers that dropped down to her ankles, and her hair was pulled back in the same fashion that Antonio pulled his into a ponytail.

Meanwhile, Antonio grabbed a shatterstone pick and hand shovel from the car and moved swiftly toward the edge of the road, instructing everyone to follow him to a flat patch of grassland below it. All stopped when he turned around. He dropped the tools on the grass and said, "This space is high enough from the lagoon and safe from the farmers who cultivate this area." His hands indicated that they form a wide circle around him.

He nodded to Isabel, who pulled out a bottle of *chicha*, some of which she poured onto the ground. His eyes were riveted to that space. He nodded and exclaimed in Quechua, "With your permission, Taita Inti, Mama Quilla, Pachamama, land of the Qanchis and our ancestors, we want to leave something in this hallowed ground, offering chicha and coca leaves in your honor. Embrace us; bless us."

He swung the pick downward to break the hard terrain while Rafael removed rocks and soil with the shovel. When the hole was deep enough, Antonio extracted Bolívar's letter from his shirt pocket and read it in Quechua and in Spanish while David translated in English.

> I, Simón Bolívar, Liberator of the Republic of Colombia, a native of the city of Caracas, in the Department of Venezuela, declare and order that, once deceased, my heart be transferred to the people of Cuzco, as proof of my true affection, even in my

last moments, for the heirs of the kingdom of the sun.
December 10, 1830.

Waving it above his head, Antonio added, "Grandfather Juan Bautista, we bring you Bolívar's answer. It took him two centuries to answer your letter of May 15, 1825, and though his physical heart no longer exists, he ensured that this letter was received by me and Isabel, your descendants, who deliver it to you."

He paused and looked down, surrounded by a sobering silence. He added, "Simón Bolívar once said that gratitude is one of the most powerful virtues anyone can possess. So, with great gratitude for the sacrifices that you, Juan Bautista Condorcanqui Túpac Amaru, made for us, and in the name of Simón Bolívar, who continues to fight for our freedom, we're burying this letter in Pomacanchi, where your house was burnt to the ground and salt was poured over it."

He wrapped Bolívar's letter in a colorful Quechuan cloth, buried it, and poured chicha and coca leaves on the ground while he said another prayer.

Appendix A

SIMÓN BOLÍVAR

Bolívar was the dean of a new vision for Latin America. By the time he wrote his letter from Jamaica in 1815 at the age of thirty-two years, he knew that incredible sufferings over three hundred years of Spanish occupation had resulted in new challenges and choices that required a steely determination on Latin America's part in favor of liberation. Intended for England but largely ignored by the English, the letter energized our space and the people who inhabited that space because of its prophetic impact. The letter affirmed the abolition of slavery, the creation of the Panama Canal, the formation of an organization of American states, and an invitation to Europe to contribute to the freedom of the Americas to bring economic equality in the world.

To the Spanish, Bolívar was as fatal with his writings as with his sword. In addition to his enormous literary output, he covered more territory in the name of freedom than anyone else in history. His moral example and military genius taught us that "a man only is defeated who accepts defeat." As a result, we carved out five new nations: Venezuela, Colombia, Perú, Ecuador, and Bolivia.

Bolívar drew strength from models like George Washington (d. 1799), Thomas Jefferson (d. 1826), and Marquis de Lafayette (d. 1834), who, although different in temperament and education, like Bolívar, were not prepared for the great feat of leading their respective countries or regions into a new age. So when Washington's family gifted Bolívar with a gold medal coined for Washington after the capitulation of the British at Yorktown, he felt deeply honored. Washington's portrait and his Yorktown medal were found among Bolívar's belongings when he died.

In spite of the influence of the Age of Enlightenment and the chain reaction it caused, with the United States leading the way toward a more democratic form of government, Bolívar felt that tyranny and anarchy would be managed best in Latin America with an authoritarian form of government. He wasn't Napoleon, he admitted. He had no dynastic ambitions, he said. He wasn't foolish either, adding, "My enemies and my foolish friends have talked so much about this crown that I will be expelled from Colombia and America." This emperor without a crown, as he was called by some, wasn't reckless. He understood that the future called for a different state of being. "Glory does not imply command," he said, "but the practice of great virtue. I wanted freedom and fame; I have achieved both. What else can I wish?"

Born Bolívar José Antonio de la Santísima Trinidad in Caracas, Venezuela, on July 24, 1783, this man called us to open ourselves to a profound experience in a play whose characters were screaming for authenticity. Bolívar had an ability to see things connected beyond the boundaries of the physical world. He ignored the symptoms of a powerless people, enticing us to become a confederation of nations, an unrecognizable reality that challenged our will. So today the search for the real Bolívar always crosses time-space boundaries and brings events, memories, and people in different countries together, many voices, part real and part absurd.

By the end of his life, he had survived twelve known assassination attempts, four of which occurred in 1828. Diverse ecosystems, histories, temperaments, and accompanying conditions like hunger, corruption, jealousies, intrigues, ignorance, and poverty that festered for centuries came to a culmination with the attempt against his life in his beloved Bogotá less than two years before his death. He was the head of a divided house breaking away from a bondage imposed through inflexibility, ambition, vengefulness, and greed. His deep moral wound, nonetheless, seeped through when he said, "They have destroyed my heart." He was referring to the plot of September 25, 1828. He physically survived the assault intact but never recovered from it emotionally.

This very complex Venezuelan man, lauded as poet, soldier, and statesman, who inspired and led us into combat against the most powerful empire of Europe, who stood atop the Andes on his way to Cuzco in 1825, was forced into exile away from the epicenter of his command forever in early May 1830. From Bogotá he journeyed through the hot plains of the Magdalena River on his way to the coast, where he planned to board an English ship in Cartagena. By the time he reached the thermal waters of Turbaco, he was a living skeleton. From Turbaco, he went to Soledad and then to Barranquilla, and from there he went on to Santa Marta because of his failing health.

Ironically, when Bolívar arrived in Colombia at the end of 1812, he bypassed Santa Marta without conceiving that eighteen years later, his exile toward Europe would take a detour to that city.

This most creative strategist who destroyed the Spanish empire in five countries, who alarmed and stunned many of his time, died in an old, torn shirt in a hacienda in the outskirts of Santa Marta that belonged to Joaquin Mier, a Spaniard turned patriot who served as Bolívar's host. Bolívar's body was carried back to Santa Marta in a simple hammock strung from a long tree pole, shouldered by men who followed a trail flanked by tamarind, saman, and pereguetano trees along the Manzanares River. His remains were embalmed with only lime and beeswax in the Casa de la Aduana and dressed in a borrowed general's shirt.

The Casa de la Aduana was a well-built structure, originally built as a one-story building by Rodrigo Bastidas, the city's founder. The house served as the consulate of Spain when owned by Joaquin Mier. It was later named the Casa de la Velación, where Bolívar was laid in state for the visitors who said their last farewell.

Ten days before he died, he spent an afternoon with his two great life companions, a hammock and tamarind trees in front of the hacienda, remembering his life, loves, and struggles. He didn't suspect that Anne Lenoit, a woman of French descent from Salamina, Colombia, whom he had met shortly after his arrival in 1812, was searching for him. When she heard that he was on his way to Europe, she had hurried behind but missed him in Cartagena, Turbaco, Soledad, and Barranquilla, arriving at the hacienda only hours after he died.

"No woman has loved him as I have!" she exclaimed as she sobbed over his body. She was the "Woman in Black" who participated in the two-hour funeral march to the cathedral.

Seven days before his death, he dictated his last will and testament among other documents. His letter bequeathing his heart to the people of Cuzco, so the story is told, was consistent with events. Morally wounded by the Colombians' conspiracy in the attempt of September 25, by the Venezuelans' refusal to allow him to return to Caracas to die there, and by the assassination of his beloved Antonio José de Sucre by a group composed of Colombians and Venezuelans, he recalled his trip through the country of the Quechua and Aymara people. In 1825, the city of Cuzco commissioned eighty gold and fifty silver medals in his honor in the same way the people of Yorktown coined the gold medal to honor George Washington. The Cuzco medal shows a profile of Bolívar on one side and the sun over a temple and a Quechua Indian in the background on the other side.

Today an example of this medal is kept by the Boston Athenaeum. The medal once belonged to General John Devereux, a member of Bolívar's Irish Legion, which was originally manned by more than two thousand Irish veterans of the Napoleonic Wars. In 1846, General Devereux gifted his medal to Thomas Handasyd Perkins, a benefactor of the Athenaeum, whose family deeded it to the Athenaeum in 1948.

Bolívar was a highly intuitive man who probably knew how his response to the last Incan king would play out some day. "I have achieved no other good than independence. That was my mission," Bolívar admitted. "The nations I have founded will, after a prolonged and bitter agony, go into an eclipse, but will later emerge states of the one great Republic, America."

ABOUT THE AUTHOR

Margaret Donnelly has pursued many historical and humanitarian objectives in each of her books. Her literary work includes four historical novels on important issues that impact the Americas. Her fourth novel, "Bolivar's Heart" (AuthorHouse Publishing) is the basis of an award-winning Mexico-US movie (*El Corazón de Bolivar*) on human trafficking. See *El corazón de Bolívar trailer (la película)* in You Tube.

In recognition of her global community work with indigenous peoples of the Americas, she was nominated for the 2004 Prize of The Right Livelihood Foundation of Sweden, known as the alternative Nobel Peace Prize. In 2007, she received the President's Community Service Award from the League of United American Citizens (LULAC) of the United States. Her second novel, "The Song of the Goldencocks" (Trafford Publishing) received an honorable mention for best historical novel at the 2007 International Latino Book Awards, Book Expo, New York City. She is a frequent public speaker and was recently interviewed by various TV channels, including Milenio and the House of Representatives of Mexico channel in Mexico City.

Margaret Donnelly received her Doctor of Jurisprudence degree in 1976 and her Bachelor of Arts degree in Latin American Studies in 1971 from the University of Texas at Austin. She is an Emeritus Attorney at Law of Texas. Her weekly column, "The Latest in Immigration," for La Estrella, a part of the Fort Worth Star Telegram, informed the North Texas community of the latest news about U.S. immigration law for many years.

Printed in the United States
By Bookmasters